THE VODKA TRAIL

by A.A. Abbott

A·A·Abbott

Copyright © 2016 A.A. Abbott

This novel is entirely a work of fiction. With the exception of lawyer Katherine Evans, the names, characters and incidents portrayed in it are a product of the author's imagination. So, alas, is the wonder drug, darria. Any other resemblance to actual persons, living or dead, or real events, is entirely coincidental.

A.A. Abbott asserts the moral right to be identified as the author of this work.

Published by Perfect City Press.

ISBN 978-0-9929621-2-8

A FEW WORDS FROM THE AUTHOR

It's been a momentous year, and I miss three beautiful souls who can never read this book: Liz Ascott, Eileen Elsey, and Linda Wilson. I thank them for being part of my life.

Thanks also to everyone who helped me turn The Vodka Trail from a simple idea into an exciting thriller.

Thanks to you, too, for picking up this book – enjoy it!

A.A. Abbott

BY A.A. ABBOTT

Up In Smoke

After The Interview

The Bride's Trail

The Vodka Trail

*See **http://aaabbott.co.uk** for my blog, free short stories and more. Sign up for my newsletter to receive freebies.*

*Follow me on Twitter **@AAAbbottStories** and **Facebook**.*

Contents

Prologue - 1991

Marty skidded his battered silver Triumph Bonneville to a halt in front of the boxy concrete building. Removing his helmet, he shook his curly blond hair out of his eyes so he could read the red Cyrillic letters above the rusty metal door: Kireniat Number Three Vodka Factory. Now the motorbike was stationary, he was aware of the late summer heat, the sweat starting to trickle onto his upper lip.

The young policeman who had been slouched in the entrance suddenly looked interested. He dropped his cigarette, reaching instead for the AK-47 semi-automatic rifle strapped across his chest.

Marty was quicker. He took two ten dollar bills from his pocket, flourishing them as he approached the man. In his best Russian, painstakingly learned, he said, "Ten dollars if you tell Mr Alexander Belov I'm here. And another ten if my bike's untouched after I've met him."

"One moment." The policeman took one of the notes. His accent was thick. That, and his stocky, swarthy appearance marked him out as a Bazaki rather than a Russian incomer. He probably claimed descent from the Mongol hordes who had swept through Bazakistan centuries before.

"Mr Belov's expecting me," Marty added, in case the young man saw an easy target for a shake-down. He wasn't afraid. While he didn't have a gun, he had a knife, and his fists; most of all, he had the swift reactions of an amateur boxer. Up close and personal, he could lay any man out cold before his adversary had the chance to shoot.

The policeman opened the door and disappeared inside, returning with another man wearing the khaki overalls of a factory worker. Tall, thin and pale, the face below his short, black spiky hair was unlined. Marty, not quite thirty himself, supposed they were around the same age.

"I'm Alexander Belov," the man said, in English. "Welcome to Kireniat." He offered his right hand to shake Marty's, pointing with his left to the flaxen-haired toddler clinging to his leg. "Don't mind my daughter, Katya. She follows me everywhere."

"It's no problem at all. I have three of my own, and another on the way," Marty said. "Your English is good."

Belov smiled. "Thank you." He was clearly flattered. "I see the West as an opportunity for me."

7

"As the East is for me," Marty said. "I'm keen to work with you to our mutual advantage." He'd taken a big risk, leaving his business in Birmingham unattended to travel to this former outpost of the Soviet Union. It had cost time and money he could barely afford.

Belov nodded. "We will be brothers." His handshake was firm. "Together, we can sell Bazaki vodka in the West. Capitalism is new to me. I know nothing of marketing, only making. But the President wants Bazakistan to learn. This country needs foreign currency."

Marty had seen the evidence of that, in the petrol and food shortages that Belov had mentioned when they'd exchanged telexes. "I'll pay you in dollars," he said. He'd brought plenty with him, prepared to buy vodka on the spot if necessary.

"Would you like to see my factory?" Belov asked eagerly.

"Yes, and taste the product," Marty said. Belov had sent samples which he'd had analysed for purity; they were fine, but the only way to be sure was to take vodka from the production line.

"Very good." Belov clapped an arm around Marty's shoulder, ushering him inside. His obvious excitement was encouraging.

Little Katya shadowed her father. She looked up at Marty, an enigmatic expression in her wide green eyes.

Chapter 1 **Kat**

Orphaned and destitute at the age of sixteen, desperate to scratch a living, Kat had made some bad decisions. She'd narrowly avoided a criminal record, and although that was luck of a sort, nothing could fill the yawning chasm that had opened in her life when her parents died. Love, security, and even her future had vanished. She'd imagined her father's business would be hers, but at the stroke of a clerk's pen, it was taken away. Now, nearly twenty-five and ready to follow her ambitions, she wanted it back.

Ross could give her the means. He was prosperous enough to pay lawyers to wrest the factory from its current owners. That wouldn't happen without a fight, probably an expensive battle through the Bazaki courts, but she was sure Ross' pockets were deep enough.

She'd made an effort for him tonight. There was champagne in the fridge and candles flickered in the master bedroom. Kat wore nothing but a wispy negligée. The eau-de-nil silk clung to her curves and highlighted her jade-green eyes. "Because you're worth it, Ross," she whispered to herself.

That wasn't the whole truth. Yes, Ross was rich, handsome and fit. His penthouse flat in Fitzrovia was perfect, set in a quiet residential street a stone's throw from London's busiest shops and bars. His generosity was lavish: flowers, designer dresses, holidays, and now the huge diamond ring that sparkled on her finger. Yet Kat didn't want to be a trophy wife. She craved independence and success in her own right, and knew she was capable of running a vodka business. That was only going to happen with Ross' help, though. Did he care about her dreams? She was about to find out.

It was after ten when Ross returned. "You're a sight for sore eyes," he said. "That dinner was so tedious."

"You went to Sketch," Kat said, puzzled. "At those prices, it should have been wonderful. I only wish I could go there myself." She twisted tendrils of her long blonde hair around her fingers.

Ross laughed. "I'll take you, then. The food was out of this world, and the wine to die for. You'd love it. I just wish I'd paid the bill myself and taken you. I only agreed to go because Wheldons are the best head hunters in the business. When they invite you to a meeting, you don't say no."

"I didn't know you were looking for another job," she said. "I thought you liked working for Davey Saxton."

Ross shrugged. "Yes, he's a nice guy, but whether I like my boss or not isn't important. He pays me well, which is what matters. Wheldons didn't have anything to tempt me, as it happens. The money wasn't enough. Anyway, if I stick around, I'll have Davey Saxton's job one day."

Kat believed him. He was clever. It was reassuring to know that, while her fiancé was already wealthy, he would be even richer in future. "Champagne?" she offered.

"You read my mind," Ross replied.

She went to the kitchen, expertly caught the cork with a towel as she opened the bottle, and poured the effervescent liquid into crystal glasses. "Cheers," she said. "We've been together exactly eight months. Let's celebrate!"

He clinked his glass against hers without returning the toast. "Did I mention I'm off to a conference in Birmingham next week?" he asked.

"No." Kat knew she would have remembered. As a teenager, she'd lived there briefly, training as a croupier before setting off to London to seek her fortune. Her brother, Erik, was working on a cancer cure in his laboratory near the centre. To cap it all, it was in the city's plush Malmaison hotel that she and Ross had spent their first night together. Should she return with him next week? It was months since she'd seen her brother. She was briefly tempted, until she realised Erik would try to dissuade her from following her dream. Worse, her brother would also do his best to deter Ross from helping her.

Ross switched on his iPad.

"Hang on," Kat said, "before you start playing poker again, I want to tell you what's on my mind."

He frowned. "Can it wait, darling? There's a tournament about to start. I should make a few thou from it, tax-free."

"It won't take me long," Kat said. "Remember what I told you about Snow Mountain vodka? It was my family business, and I want it back." Despite the years that had passed, she resented the injustice that had led to her father's imprisonment, the distillery's seizure, and ultimately her parents' deaths. Ross needed to understand what it meant to her. "Will you help me?"

Ross frowned. "I'd rather you forgot all about Bazakistan. Frankly, I thought you'd want to, after…"

She interrupted. "After what happened to my parents?"

Ross reached out and took her hand. He stroked the diamond as the stone sparkled in the candlelight. "I don't want you to be reminded of the past, darling. Anyway what can I do? I'm an actuary, not a distiller or even a lawyer. You could ask Ted, of course. He's the best lawyer I know. Personally, I think your chances are slim. The factory's in a country with a less developed legal system than the UK. I'd rather you focused on planning our wedding – and the honeymoon."

There was a mischievous glint in his blue eyes. He began to caress her arm, reaching through the negligée up to her shoulder.

Kat pulled away from him. "I'll ring Ted tomorrow, then." She'd make sure he sent the bill to Ross. She added, eyes flashing, "I was brought up to run the distillery. I could do so much to make Snow Mountain a big name brand. Marty Bridges doesn't market it properly."

Ross started to untie her silk garment. He seemed to have decided that poker could wait. "You're not a marketing expert yourself, darling, are you? I suppose you could ask that girl who shared your flat. Amy, wasn't it?"

"Amy works for Marty Bridges, with my brother," Kat said, exasperated. "They're crazy. The man's a snake."

"I love you when you're angry," Ross murmured, apparently serious. "Drink your champagne." He kissed her lightly on the lips.

It was hard to resist him. As his deep blue eyes gazed into hers, Kat responded to his kisses. There would be plenty of time to pursue her plans in the morning.

Chapter 2 **Marty**

Marty was proud of his silver Jaguar F-Type. It was locally made, swift and showy, a symbol of his success. As he parked by the Rose Villa Tavern, he was satisfied that his car outclassed the others lining Warstone Lane.

The pub was a gabled red brick structure dwarfed by the white oblong next to it. This was the Big Peg, a huge office building. Marty thought it out of place amid the Victorian architecture of Birmingham's Jewellery Quarter, but it had its uses; offices within it were often advertised for letting, a convenient benchmark for the properties he owned in the area.

Marty was late, and reflected that it was fortunate Erik had a placid nature like his father. The young man wouldn't be watching the clock, although he'd be halfway through a pint already. The converted jewellery workshop where Erik worked on their joint venture was just a few minutes' walk from the pub, after all.

To Marty's surprise, however, his business partner was nowhere in sight. Instead, Marty spied Amy in a lively discussion with a man he recognised as her father, Charles.

They were sitting in the old-fashioned leather armchairs that dominated the little snug off the bar. Amy had a cocktail in front of her. She was twisting a strand of her long, copper-coloured hair around her fingers, frowning as she spoke. Charles, listening avidly, was drinking real ale. Marty approved.

He ordered his beer, overhearing Charles say, "It's profits that pay all our wages."

"Telling the wench what's what, are we?" Marty said, placing a hand on Charles' shoulder.

Amy blushed and looked away. Marty wondered what she'd been saying about him.

"Amy was just telling me all about your cancer research," Charles said. "It sounds like you have a blockbuster drug on your hands."

"I believe so," Marty agreed. "My partner could say more about how it works. He's synthesised the active ingredient from darria, a shrub that's reputed to have anti-ageing properties. My wife certainly believes in it. She drinks darria tea every day." Angela had tried to inflict it on him too, but so far, he'd won that battle. It wasn't as if the tea would bring hair back to his bald patch, or return his physique to the athleticism of youth.

He added, "Clinical trials on darria extract have been promising, but of course, marketing is key in deciding on the next phase." He nodded at Amy. "You'd find it hard to believe darria was a wonder shrub if you tripped over it. It's a twiggy little thing, nothing to look at. You wouldn't bother growing it in your garden."

"Dad doesn't have a garden," Amy said. "He's got a flat in Shoreditch."

"It used to be a rough part of London, but no longer," Charles said. "It's handy for my work in the City, and good for bars, too. New ones are opening all the time."

"That's similar to the Jewellery Quarter," Marty said. In his youth, it had been crammed with metal-bashers and artisan workshops. His first wife's wedding ring had been made there. Rather than try one of the shops on Vyse Street, with their tempting displays of gold, he'd taken her to a workshop where her finger was measured and the ring priced by weight.

"This is a great place to live," Amy said, adding swiftly, "And work."

"What brings you to Birmingham?" Marty asked Charles. He knew Amy rarely saw her parents. Charles had visited the city only once before, when he'd as good as interviewed Marty and Erik before Amy accepted their job offer.

"I'm at an insurance conference for a couple of days," Charles said.

Marty whistled. "Sounds exciting."

"It will be," Charles said. "I'm running a workshop on cyber security."

"Dad's not ashamed of his inner geek," Amy said.

"The hottest ticket in town, no doubt," Marty said. "Glad to see you supping a local brew, meanwhile. If you want to try some more later, come with me. My wife's out with the girls tonight, so I've got a pass for the evening." He wagged a finger theatrically at Amy. "You'll be needing an early night, bab. I'm expecting to see you bright-eyed with those market research results first thing tomorrow."

A waitress brought burgers to Charles and Amy. Marty looked at them longingly. "I think I'll order one myself," he said. "My wife's insisted I join her on the five:two diet. Yesterday was a fast day, so I need to catch up on my calories." He winked. "I can't allow the diet to work, or she'll keep me on it forever."

"I highly recommend the chips," Charles said.

13

"I'm definitely having them," Marty said. He studied the other man, noting that Charles was in good shape despite the chips and beer. His figure was trim and his face youthful, only a few laughter lines radiating from his eyes, and his short back and sides still dark. With a twenty-three-year-old daughter, he must be in his early forties at least. Marty thought ruefully of the image in his own mirror: a rotund middle-aged man with a horseshoe of grey hair circling his pate. He didn't need darria tea, he needed a miracle.

Erik arrived just as Marty had chosen from the menu. Marty ordered food for both of them and bought more beer. They settled into seats around the corner from Amy and Charles, beneath a semi-circular stained glass window. The nineteenth century bones of the pub had been polished, painted and wallpapered with birds and flowers. As well as the real ale clips, there was an excellent selection of vodkas. Snow Mountain wasn't one of them, and Marty made a mental note to speak to the manager again.

"Busy day?" Marty asked.

"I wanted to process some results before our brainstorming meeting tomorrow," Erik said.

"I'm looking forward to it," Marty said. "Let's have Amy present her market research first, then we can talk about next steps for the business. We should review costs as well. I've been running financial projections and I'll share them with you." He wished Erik would focus on cash too; darria wasn't bringing in an income, yet the overheads of developing it were high. There were outlays for running an office, clinical trials and market research, as well as Erik and Amy's wages.

Erik's response was enthusiastic, although he totally ignored the monetary aspects of the project. Green eyes animated, he started describing improvements he'd made in extracting darria's essence from the shrub. He looked so like his father at the same age that Marty blinked once or twice. Erik could have been Alexander Belov, or Sasha as Marty had learned to call him, spelling out the purity of his vodka.

A drink with Erik was always just that, of course, not a long session in the pub. After a pint and a burger, he rose to leave.

"I'll just see if Amy wants a lift back," Marty said.

"Is she here?" Erik's eyes softened.

Marty jerked a thumb at the snug. "With her father. I'm going to take him out, show him the sights. Well, a decent pub or two, anyway."

Amy and Charles were just finishing brownies.

"On expenses?" Marty asked, tongue in cheek.

"How did you guess?" Charles flashed him a grin. Noticing Erik, he shook the young man's hand. "I'm glad to hear Amy's enjoying working with you. I hear your office isn't far."

"My flat isn't either," Amy said. "I don't need a lift, Marty; it's a short walk home."

"I'm going there too," Erik said. "I'll walk back with you, Amy."

Charles looked askance at both of them, and Marty felt obliged to put him right. "They each have a studio flat above the office in Leopold Passage. The only way I could get planning permission for that old workshop was to create live-work units in it."

"No expense spared," Erik joked. "We painted the walls ourselves."

"Your flats are exactly as you like them, then," Marty said. "Ready, Charles? Let's head for the White Horse." He was grateful for an excuse. It was near his social club and he might wander down there later.

They left the Rose Villa Tavern, Charles gratefully drawing on a cigarette. "My Jag's over here," Marty told Charles. "It'll only be a ten minute drive. Just for once, the Council aren't digging up the roads."

He'd hoped Charles would have a compliment or two for the car, but the Londoner strapped himself into its passenger seat without a word.

"What do you drive?" Marty asked.

"A Porsche 911 Turbo," Charles replied.

That took the shine off Marty's Jag. "Very nice," he said. It wasn't what he expected of an IT professional; insurance must pay well. Once he'd turned the key in the Jag's ignition, he made sure to accelerate as quickly as possible.

The White Horse was another red brick building, rather smaller and set squarely in suburbia near a medical centre and neat rows of houses. Marty parked on the street and led Charles inside. A computer monitor on the bar announced the beers available, their prices, style and strength. Marty paid it no heed.

"Is the Bathams on?" Marty asked the young barmaid. "All right, two pints please, bab."

"Hang on, I haven't chosen yet," Charles said, sounding discomfited.

"Trust me, you don't have to," Marty said. "If they've got Bathams, there's no need to drink anything else." He nodded to the barmaid. "Carry on, bab."

Charles sipped the amber drink thoughtfully. "It's superb," he acknowledged.

"It's called Bathams Best Bitter for a reason," Marty said. "It's brewed a few miles away." He couldn't help feeling smug. Evidently, the ale didn't travel as far as London.

"Not one of your products, then," Charles said. "You sell Snow Mountain vodka, don't you? There isn't any here and I didn't see it at the Rose Villa Tavern either."

"I would like to get it into the tavern, I must confess," Marty said. "They have a reputation for selling high-end vodkas similar to Snow Mountain. Currently, they're stocking my competitors, but I'm working on it." He grinned. "Vodka's not the only way to turn a profit. I have high hopes for your Amy's ideas for our cancer-busting tea."

"Marty Bridges, saviour of the NHS," Charles said.

"Hardly," Marty said modestly. "Even when your cancer's beaten, you smokers will die of something else. We've all got to go one day. Anyway, there's plenty to do before I put that tea on sale. I need a supply of darria for starters. I'm off to Bazakistan soon to buy up land for a plantation."

"Bazakistan," Charles mused. "What a coincidence. It must be a land of opportunity. One of my colleagues at Saxton Brown wants to do business there. You remember Ross Pritchard?"

"Really?" Marty pricked up his ears. He'd met Ross a couple of times. The young man had failed to impress. He'd been to public school, and thought a lot of himself. His interest in Erik's sister, Kat, bordered on an obsession. Of course, she took full advantage of it.

While Marty was unconvinced of Ross' merits, he had even less time for Kat. He was certain her fiancé's appeal lay in his wealth. Unlike Erik, she still hankered for the opulent lifestyle she'd enjoyed when her parents owned the vodka distillery in Bazakistan.

Marty sighed. What had happened to Kat and Erik's parents was unconscionable, but he'd been unable to stop it at the time and he couldn't turn back the clock now. She should accept that the vodka factory was part of her past, not her future. If she thought she could use Ross' cash to wrest the distillery from its current owner, she was sadly mistaken. That wasn't how Bazakistan worked. While money talked, political influence shouted louder.

He tried to find out more from Charles. "Most people don't even know where Bazakistan is. What are Ross' plans?"

Charles didn't answer the question. "It's pretty corrupt there, isn't it?" he said. "I doubt I'd go there myself."

"I've often visited to arrange vodka shipments," Marty said. "It's the kind of place you can do business. Low on red tape. Politically stable. The President's held down his job for a long time."

"So I hear," Charles said. "He must be an old man. Who knows who will succeed him? He probably shot them all. At any rate, other countries in the region are volatile. Violence could spill over into Bazakistan at any time. I told Ross not to go there. You've got travel insurance, I assume?"

"Of course," Marty replied, allowing a self-satisfied expression to settle on his face.

"And kidnap, key man and business interruption insurance?"

"No." Marty could tell the hard sell was on its way. He lifted his pint and took a draught.

"We can give you a good rate at Saxton Brown."

"Aren't you an IT bod?" Marty asked, amused at Charles' cheek. "How is it you're giving me a sales pitch?"

Charles smiled. "Our products would be useful to you. I'd be letting you down if I didn't tell you about them."

"I've never had key man insurance, but I need it," Marty said thoughtfully. "If anything happened to Erik, the darria joint venture would go pear-shaped. His research is all written down, of course, but that guy carries so much knowledge in his head. I'm always telling him evidence is everything." He tutted. "Erik knows I'm right."

"You should look at kidnap insurance as well," Charles said. "You travel to places that others wouldn't. Listen, the more products you take as a bundle, the better the rate we can give you."

"Like cable TV?" Marty said. "Okay, but I'll be shopping around. Let me know your best price, and I'll be expecting mates' rates. And it's your round." He held out his empty glass.

Charles took the hint. "Want another Bathams?" he asked.

"Don't mind if I do," Marty said.

Charles bought the beers. "The least I can do for a valued customer, and Amy's boss," he said. "She seems to have settled in quickly. I've heard all about her job. She knows her way around Birmingham, too."

"Especially the bars," Marty said. "My youngest daughter has been helping her there." The two girls were a similar age and had become friends.

"How many children do you have?" Charles asked.

"Four. All except my youngest work for me," Marty said, taking a swig. "It keeps them on the straight and narrow, but it's a constant reminder that being a father doesn't stop once the kids are grown up. You'd know that too, of course. How many do you have?"

Charles said nothing.

Marty's curiosity was piqued. He'd asked only out of politeness. Amy's family wasn't a matter of concern to him, and he'd certainly never quizzed her about it. Still, this wasn't the reaction he'd expected. "Out with it," he said. "What ails you?"

"Amy's an only child," Charles said. "I think."

"You mean you're not sure?" Marty asked, wondering why Charles was so coy about it.

Charles looked embarrassed. "Amy suspects my ex is pregnant. Look." He tapped at his smartphone.

The screen sprang to life. A gorgeous blonde smiled at them. "Hi, I'm Dee," she said, flicking her long, honey-coloured locks from her lightly tanned face. "Are you pregnant? Lacking in energy or worried about the birth? Suppose you could wave a magic wand and solve everything? Well, I've got the next best thing for you, and it's yoga."

"An online yoga course for mums-to-be," Charles said.

"Hold on," Marty said. "That's Dee Saxton, isn't it? My wife used her online meditation lessons. Is she Amy's mother?"

"Er, no," Charles said sheepishly. "I've been divorced for a while. Dee's my ex-girlfriend. I rushed into a relationship with her. Amy didn't approve at all. She called Dee my mid-life crisis girlfriend."

"My kids were the same with Angela, my second wife," Marty said sympathetically. "She's not their mum, you see. I told them I couldn't bring her back from the dead."

"Sorry to hear…" Charles began.

"It was a car crash," Marty said. "One of those things." He didn't wish to dwell on it. "You were saying?"

"I thought I'd been too hasty, so I moved out." Charles sighed. "That was a big mistake. Even Amy says that now. I just wanted more space and I'd planned to carry on seeing her. Dee wasn't having any of it. I had no idea she was expecting a baby."

"You still don't know if she is, or if it's yours," Marty said, thinking Charles a fool to walk out on a cracker like Dee.

Charles fiddled in his pocket, his expression gloomy. "I could use another cigarette, Marty."

"I'll come outside with you," Marty said. He didn't want more beer. Charles had almost certainly had too much already. The man surely wouldn't have confided in him otherwise. They hardly knew each other.

They sat on the smokers' benches in front of the pub. Charles lit a Marlboro. He was obviously highly strung; no wonder he smoked so much.

Marty filled the silence. "It's up to you whether you ask your ex. Secrets and lies will out eventually. That's all I'll say." He finished his bitter. "I should be getting back. I'll give you a lift."

"But you've had at least three pints," Charles protested. "You'll be over the limit."

Marty considered his words. The chances of encountering the police were slim. "No worries," he said. "I can handle my drink. Anyway, the last time I was breathalysed, they lost the paperwork."

"That was lucky," Charles said.

Marty chortled. He was sure being a mason had helped. "I make my own luck," he told Charles.

Chapter 3 **Davey**

Davey Saxton's routine didn't change just because he was at a conference. Always an early riser, he'd made a coffee and was watching dawn break outside his hotel window.

When the phone rang, he registered the caller's name with surprise. Alana Green was the CEO of Bishopstoke, the company that had bought Veritable Insurance the year before. That had led to Davey's departure from the top job at Veritable. As expected, given her aggressive reputation, Alana had fired him as soon as the takeover deal was signed. When she'd tried to buy part of the business of his new company, Saxton Brown, he'd told her where to go.

"Good morning, Davey." Alana's American accent was unmistakable. "I was planning to clear my head with a jog around the canals. Would you care to join me?"

"I thought you'd still be tucked up in bed at five thirty," Davey said.

Alana snorted. "Sleep is for wimps." She added, "I'd feel safer with a man. I'm looking out of my window at those towpaths. They're deserted."

Davey laughed, flattered. "This is Birmingham, you know, not Harlem. Still, if it makes you feel better, I'll meet you in the lobby in five." He'd rather imagined Alana could take care of herself; indeed, that any low-life pulling a knife on her would find themselves pitched straight into the canal below.

He didn't ask where she was staying. Everybody who was anybody in the insurance world was booked into the Hyatt for the conference. Bishopstoke alone probably had twenty executives in the shiny black tower. Davey, Ross and Charles had struggled to secure rooms, remaining on the waiting list until the week before.

Davey whistled, enjoying the view of central Birmingham as the glass-sided lift descended twenty-one floors. A breath of fresh air would be a pleasant start to the day. He'd been about to go to the gym, anyway, and now he might hear some industry gossip. He suspected that was really why the Bishopstoke CEO wanted to see him.

At just under six foot, Alana cut a striking figure, a slim African-American with perfect posture. She was wearing a black jogging suit and trainers he recognised as Scotts, a runners' brand.

"Aren't you cold?" she asked, looking pointedly at Davey's singlet and shorts. There was still a spring chill in the morning air.

"Perhaps I should have brought a hat." Davey fingered his bald head. "I'll warm up soon enough, I guess. Shall we go?"

They left the hotel. Traffic was already clattering along the road outside. By contrast, once they'd found the red brick steps to the canal below, they were in a world of tranquillity. A ribbon of dark water reflected the bridges, brick walls and brightly coloured houseboats above its surface. The brick path next to it stretched past the International Convention Centre, under bridges and away into the distance.

"I warn you, I'm quick," Alana said. "I do this most mornings."

"I'll give you a run for your money," Davey promised. "I'm training for an Iron Man."

"That's a triathlon on steroids, isn't it?" Alana said. "Impressive."

They began to sprint alongside the Birmingham to Fazeley Canal. Davey sensed Alana was pushing herself to her limit, yet he easily matched her, with more in reserve. He allowed himself to feel a quiet sense of pride. She must be at least six years younger, an age difference that had counted against him when Bishopstoke's shareholders were deciding who should lead the merged company. Of course, he was male, even taller and longer-limbed than Alana, and exceptionally fit. He took the Iron Man challenge seriously and was training hard.

He expected to meet commuters walking into work, but the silence of the water was mirrored by the world around it. Lichen-encrusted walls and red brick buildings, three storeys high or more, towered above them. As the canal passed under long road and railway bridges, they encountered a few rough sleepers, huddled together under blankets and oblivious to the world.

Alana's lip curled. She looked away.

Davey said gently, "You needn't worry, Alana. They're out for the count. Still, I'm glad I came with you."

"Thank you." She shivered.

They left the vagrants behind, emerging into the light. After a further ten minutes, running through an area of newer and less attractive industrial buildings, Alana slowed to a halt. "I think we should go back, Davey. I've got work to do."

"Me too," he agreed. He was seeing Ross and Charles for breakfast. It was inadvisable to mention that to her. Ross had been Veritable

Insurance's smartest actuary; Davey had heard on the grapevine of Alana's irritation when Ross chose to go to Saxton Brown after the Bishopstoke takeover.

They retraced their steps. Under the bridges, Davey stopped briefly to tuck a banknote next to each sleeping head.

"It won't solve their problems," Alana said. "They'll wake up and go straight to the liquor store. I've seen losers like that back home in New York. I wasn't raised in the swankiest part of town."

"I'll take that risk," Davey said. "No one should sleep outside in a rich country like this." He asked himself if she'd really been afraid of them earlier, or if her reaction was simply distaste.

As they arrived at their hotel, Alana said, "Thank you, Davey. That was great. Could we meet again for dinner tonight?"

Davey wondered at the reason for the charm offensive. Although he caught her eye, her gaze revealed nothing. "I'd like that, Alana," he said. "None of us can possibly network enough. There's just one thing I should mention first."

She continued to display no emotion. "Yes?" she prompted.

"No part of my business is up for sale, Alana. As long as you remember that, we'll get on fine."

Chapter 4 **Marty**

Marty could have travelled to work on foot. His office was scarcely a mile from the white stucco mansion he shared with Angela. It wasn't a pleasant walk, however. The route passed through traffic-choked highways before arriving at the industrial zone where he'd bought a warehouse twenty years before. Like all his properties, he'd won it at auction for a keen price. Never overpay, never undersell; that was his motto.

He waited for the rush hour to abate before setting off in his Jag. Smooth as silk, the car hummed quietly with understated power. No policemen had stopped him the previous night and there were none in view this morning. Marty doubted he'd been over the limit when he left the White Horse, anyway. He had an extraordinary capacity for alcohol, born of years of practice. Beer barely touched the sides.

He parked the Jag in the space reserved next to his office, a single storey brick building dwarfed by the warehouse behind it. His visitors were already waiting on plastic chairs in the reception lobby, Erik in jeans as usual and Amy wearing a blue kimono and dark trousers. Marty assumed it was the fashion of the moment.

He noticed Amy look disdainfully at her surroundings. The small room could use a lick of paint, he decided. Now he'd redeveloped the workshop where the duo were based, he could see this property was looking tired. He might pop round at the weekend with a pot of paint and some new carpet tiles. The sign outside, proclaiming that East West Bridges was based here, looked shabby too. He'd titivate it if he had any paint left.

"Come on through," Marty said, punching the code that released the door to the rest of the premises. "Has Tanya offered you coffee?"

"Yes, drinks are on the way," Erik said.

Marty ushered them to his own den, a large room panelled and furnished in bird's eye maple. This, at least, needed no decorating. The cream carpet was plush and pristine. Every surface that could be polished was gleaming under the spotlights shining from the pure white ceiling. On the meeting table, there was a tray with refreshments: white china cups and teapot, cafetière, cream, milk, sugar and a plate of shortbread fingers.

Marty motioned to his colleagues to sit at two of the S-shaped black leather chairs around the table. "Milk and sugar?" he asked, pouring the drinks without waiting for a reply. He splashed extra cream into Amy's coffee, ignoring the irritation that flitted across her face. That girl needed fattening up, even if she didn't see it herself. She was thin enough to pass through a fax machine.

He took a piece of shortbread and passed the plate round. Amy took one. Marty grinned, eager to hear the results of Amy's market research. "Ready with your presentation, Amy? Anything you need?"

Amy was opening her briefcase to remove a laptop. Marty had expected her to reflect his enthusiasm, but she didn't smile. "I'm good," she said distantly. Maybe she was nervous.

He let Amy busy herself with his AV equipment. She was familiar with it, as both she and Erik had been summoned to Marty's office many times since the joint venture began. A huge monitor lurked behind one of the panelled walls. Amy jabbed the remote control. The panel slid away, revealing a screen full of white noise. "Been watching football?" she asked him.

"I couldn't possibly comment," Marty said. In truth, he rarely used it for anything else.

Amy fiddled with the remote and plugged a USB extender into her laptop. The big screen sprang into life with a picture of a patient sitting in a hospital bed. 'Darria will make a difference', the strapline proclaimed.

"And how," Marty said. "All right, bab, let death by PowerPoint commence."

Amy flicked to another slide, a frown of concentration on her face. "Here are some statistics," she said. "We carried out market research across a population of two thousand people."

"Where were they?" Marty asked. "This population? Down the road from here, perhaps."

Amy pretended to slap him. "Don't interrupt, Marty. They were all over the country. This was a UK-wide survey. One third of interviewees were well, one third were cancer patients and one third were cancer survivors. More than 99% had never heard of darria."

"What a surprise," Marty murmured.

"Indeed. And it got interesting then. I couldn't say darria was a potential cure – that's against the law – but I could ask whether they'd use a food supplement that was rumoured to beat cancer. It would be sold

24

as a tea to drink once a day. Ten per cent of cancer patients would drink it in addition to their NHS treatment. Besides, ten per cent of survivors and five per cent of people who had never had cancer would drink it to stay well."

Erik looked as if a wasp had stung him. "You asked them about tea? That's how the villagers in the valleys of Bazakistan use darria, but we're going further. We'll be launching a prescription drug."

"It'll take too long," Marty said. "And the trials are costing a fortune. Look, I'll show you a spreadsheet with costs to date and estimated outlays to completion." He reached for a laptop on his desk.

"Can I finish the presentation first?" Amy asked.

"Yes, go ahead," Marty said. "We'll discuss the cost of clinical trials later, Erik, but that was my concern when I asked Amy to research the UK market's appetite for tea."

"There's no point," Erik protested. Dismay was written on his face, but he kept his voice calm. "Marty, if you say that darria tea cures cancer, the regulators will treat it as a medicinal product. You can't sell a medicinal product without a licence, and you won't get one without clinical trials. Don't you see, Marty? There's no money to be saved, because I'm going to have to run trials anyway."

Marty had debated the same issues with his lawyer and was confident he could wriggle around the regulations. "I believe it depends how we position the product," he said. "As long as we don't advertise darria as a cancer remedy, we can register it as a food supplement. What did you tell your cast of thousands, Amy?"

"That there was a buzz about a certain brand of herbal tea, and it was reported to be a cure," Amy replied. She rapidly flicked through her slides.

"Exactly," Erik said. "Why would anyone drink it otherwise? The problem is, we can't allege it's a cancer treatment without a licence."

"No, we can't," Marty said, his patience tested. "But others can. We'll just advertise darria tea as supporting good health. That doesn't involve medicinal claims. At the same time, though, we'll run press trips to Bazakistan, all expenses paid. The journalists will meet doctors who will talk about the miracle cures they've seen with darria. They can interview centenarians too. It's a great news story." He was satisfied this was the answer.

"Yes," Amy agreed. Her eyes were shining. "It should whip up a social media storm too. Word will spread."

Erik glared at her. She looked away from him.

Erik continued with his objections. "Bazakistan's unstable," he said. "You'll have to pay bribes to keep the journalists safe from the President's militia, let alone the freedom fighters who hide out in the valleys where darria grows."

"I can afford it," Marty said. He was sanguine about paying a few bribes. The cost of the press junkets would still be modest compared with clinical trials. He turned to Amy. "Did you cover price and outlets?"

"Of course," Amy said. "Demand is relatively inelastic, with little sensitivity to price until you exceed a pound per cup. The convenience of teabags wins over leaves by an overwhelming majority, even if leaves are cheaper. The survey groups were also asked whether they'd prefer to buy online, through supermarkets, at chemists or in health food shops. Practically everyone would purchase through an online shop or a supermarket. The numbers fall dramatically for other outlets. Here's a slide that explains it." She pressed a button on her keyboard.

Erik folded his arms, face stony and voice crackling with tension. "That's enough about the tea. I think your marketing strategy's unwise and it's too dependent on viral marketing. Amy, you should have focused your market research on prescription drugs."

"We did that too," Amy said, flushing. She looked only at Marty, refusing to meet Erik's eyes. "The results were less conclusive, that's all. With a handful of exceptions, the cancer patients told us they would take anything their doctors prescribed." She shrugged. "Sadly, some patients wanted it now. We had to explain that wasn't possible at the experimental stage."

Marty was about to suggest they'd be first in line to buy darria tea. He noticed Erik's grim expression and decided against it.

"What about the rest of your sample?" Erik asked.

"The control group – those who'd never had cancer – weren't interested," Amy said. "Why would you ask for a prescription drug if you were well? Ten per cent of survivors would request a prescription to prevent recurrence, although we can't be certain doctors would prescribe it."

"They should," Erik said robustly.

"It depends if there's a preventative effect," Amy said.

"It has to be demonstrable," Marty said. "Even then, it must offer value for money too."

"It will," Erik protested. "I want to sell the drug cheaply to make it accessible to all."

"We can't sell it too cheaply, Erik," Marty pointed out. He was becoming painfully aware of his partner's lack of commercial knowledge. "We need to recover the cost of our research and make a profit on top." He wanted a fat, juicy profit. At least Amy understood that. Marty was encouraged by the prospect of healthy tea sales.

Erik evidently wasn't. He looked tense. "We mustn't make the drug so expensive that doctors won't prescribe it," he said. "Have you talked to doctors too, Amy?"

"A limited survey of cancer specialists was carried out," Amy said. "If they think it's better than the alternatives, they'll prescribe it, whatever the cost."

Marty had heard enough. "Why bother with the drug? There's a massive demand for darria tea," he said. "We've got to start production as soon as possible. I'm going to get on a plane to Bazakistan and buy up a darria plantation."

Erik glowered. "You agreed to fund my drug research," the younger man said, his tone uncharacteristically angry. "Tea won't solve anything. I'm not convinced your viral marketing will work. Even if it does, cancer sufferers won't drink enough to cure themselves, especially if you charge a pound a cup."

Marty stood his ground. "Erik, the market research proves otherwise. Customers will invest in their own health. What's the point of distilling the shrub into a prescription drug as well? Doctors won't prescribe it if their patients can simply drink tea."

Amy, glancing anxiously at both of them, opened her mouth to speak. Erik interrupted before she could say a word. "Marty, I won't let you do this," he said. "If you want to get rich selling tea, you can find another partner and another product." He rose to his feet. "I'm going to see my friends at the university. I need an investor with a sense of social responsibility."

"Wait," Marty said. He'd never had an argument with the young man. Erik was pragmatic and inclined to seek common ground.

This time, it was different. Erik turned his back on both of them. He walked out.

Marty stared at the open door, noting that Amy looked shocked too.

"How come Erik didn't know how the market research was progressing?" he asked. "You both work in the same office."

Amy squirmed. "Erik's usually in the lab. Even in the office, he's totally focused on science." She chewed her lip. "I was afraid he wouldn't like what I had to say."

"You weren't wrong." Marty admitted to himself that he hadn't appreciated the strength of Erik's moral stance. He'd imagined the logic of a cost-benefit analysis would speak for itself, even though Erik had made it clear he wasn't interested in finance. Amy seemed to understand the young man better. "Tell me what you'd do in my shoes," he asked.

"Listen to Erik," she said hotly. "It's the least you can do after the years of work he's put into this, the long hours in the lab every day. Darria is his life."

"And my investment, which I want to recoup," Marty reminded her. "Besides, we can't continue with only a small lab and shoestring staff. Despite what Erik thinks, I know the rules. I'd have to spend much more to bring a prescription drug to market."

"The answer's obvious, then," Amy said. "Doctors will prescribe a drug if it works. What's the problem with launching darria tea and continuing with Erik's research?"

"Only money," Marty replied.

"You won't lose out," Amy said. "The tea sales will fund the research. Once the drug's launched as well, you'll have two revenue streams."

That sounded plausible. "You could be right," he said. "Give me a copy of your presentation, and more data if you have it. I'll crunch the numbers."

"Don't forget, my market research was limited to the UK, for reasons of cost," Amy said. "There's potential elsewhere."

"Agreed," Marty said. "Less red tape in some countries too. You can advertise drugs in America, for a start. As we're based in the UK, it made sense to test the market here first. I won't ignore the foreign upside, though."

Amy still looked stressed. "Shouldn't you ring Erik?"

"I'll do it now," Marty said, reaching for his phone.

Erik didn't reply. After listening to the voicemail greeting, Marty said, "I'm going to rework my financials, Erik. I'll almost certainly pay for your research. I'll even pay for lawyers to put that in writing. Give me a call back, please." He frowned. "I hope he'll accept that. We've got so much to do. Brand name, patent registrations, raw materials, production facilities, packaging…"

"Do you want to see the rest of my presentation?" Amy asked.

"Email me," Marty said. "I'll send everything to Katherine Evans. She's my lawyer, and she'll register the brand and make sure the patents are up to date for the tea and the drug. Erik's made tweaks to the extraction process, so we need to get that patented for a start." He stood up, stretching and yawning, keen to end the meeting. "Onwards and upwards, bab," he added.

"There's just one more thing I need to discuss," Amy said. She fiddled with her fingers. "It's a bit difficult."

"Can't it wait?" Marty asked.

"It won't take long." She was blushing again. "Marty, you and Erik don't always agree on the direction of the darria business. You're looking to make money, while he wants to bring a cancer cure to the masses. I find it difficult working for you both when I'm caught in the middle."

"Are you saying I'm wrong?" Marty demanded. He could see where her sympathies lay.

Amy shifted awkwardly in her seat. "No," she said, with apparent conviction. "A business has to generate profits. My father drummed that into me."

Despite the tension in the air, Marty grinned. "That's a good lesson to learn."

"It is," Amy conceded. "But that's the problem. I know you're right, but Erik doesn't see it."

He understood now. "You don't want to tell him, do you?"

"It isn't my job, Marty, and to be honest, my diplomatic skills aren't up to it. I can tell you both what you can sell and how you can sell it. I can't solve your arguments. Listen, I hope you like what you've seen of my work so far. If you have a marketing position in your vodka business, I'd love to do that instead."

Marty was somewhat alarmed. It was hardly a vote of confidence in his darria enterprise. Was she afraid the partners wouldn't reconcile their interests? "That came out of left field," he said. "Don't you like Erik?"

"Of course I do," Amy said. Her face was bright red.

He remembered the sudden sweetness in Erik's eyes when Amy's name had been mentioned the previous evening. "Are you seeing him?" he asked.

"No," Amy protested.

She would like to, he suspected. It showed her taste in men was improving. In the past, she'd been keen on Ross Pritchard, who had nothing to recommend him but his bank balance.

Marty grimaced. He was no agony uncle. His priority must be rebuilding his relationship with Erik. Darria had the potential to make millions for him, surpassing even the lucrative Snow Mountain vodka distribution business. Without Erik, it wouldn't happen. "I don't have another marketing job for you, Amy," he said, "but the minute there is one, I'll call you."

He moved towards the door and held it open for her. When she'd left, he tried once again to ring his business partner.

Chapter 5 **Davey**

The conference offered a variety of talks and workshops, but that wasn't why Davey and his colleagues were attending. Once he and Charles had given seminars to the other delegates, their first day passed in a whirl of networking. Saxton Brown was less than a year old, and he needed to raise its profile. Afterwards, he made an informal pitch to several insurance brokers in the hotel bar. He was drinking with them when he realised it was seven thirty, the time he'd arranged to meet Alana. Davey made excuses and dashed away, still in the charcoal suit and blue shirt he'd worn all day.

She was waiting for Davey in the hotel atrium. He'd seen her earlier in business clothes, but now she'd changed into a simple black shift and pearl choker. The dress suited her slim figure. Shiny black stilettos elongated her legs and added to her height; he was no longer looking down at her.

"That was a mind-blowing day," Davey admitted. "I need to recover my strength. Where are we going?"

"A little place about a mile away," Alana said. "We could walk, but," she gestured to her shoes, "I've booked a cab." She picked up a Louis Vuitton valise. Davey assumed it contained her laptop. He hoped she wouldn't spend half the evening checking emails.

Their taxi was already outside, a placard in the passenger window announcing GREEN. As it inched through roadworks, it occurred to Davey that it would have been quicker to walk. He looked regretfully at Alana's heels.

She stretched her ebony legs. "I thought your speech this afternoon was very interesting," she said.

"Thank you." Davey welcomed the compliment. Alana didn't give them lightly. "I think we need more niche players like mine in the London market. I wanted to let the young guns know it's possible to raise capital and set up on their own."

"It helps to have your track record," Alana pointed out.

"True," Davey acknowledged. "But it's about spotting winners too. My IT director, Charles, came from a bank. And young Ross didn't have my experience, but he's extremely able."

"The best actuary Veritable Insurance ever had," Alana said. "When I bought the company, I was sorry to see him go. I gave him a promotion, but it wasn't enough."

Davey grinned. He understood Ross too well. It was pound notes that motivated the actuary, and Davey had offered Ross more of them than Alana. Naturally, he'd make sure he kept Ross' package competitive. He didn't want Alana luring the rising star back.

Alana made small talk about the conference and the other speakers until they arrived at their destination, a Michelin-starred restaurant in a rambling white Georgian house. Dusk was falling, and candles flickered invitingly on each table. They were seated by a picture window overlooking a garden lush with greenery.

Alana ordered champagne. "It's the greatest European invention," she declared, "and I'll touch nothing else with a meal."

Davey was happy to acquiesce. He was partial to it himself and often had a glass with his wife, Laura; she said it was low in calories. "I'll split a bottle with you," Davey said, "although I enjoy a good craft beer, and I believe I should thank you Americans for persuading us it's cool."

They toasted Europe and America before choosing from a menu of delicious dishes, the prices reflecting the luxurious ingredients used. Alana selected low carbohydrate options and refused offers of bread. Davey had no such restraint. He ordered crab risotto and steak.

"We can match wines to your meal," the waitress offered.

Alana simpered at Davey. "Champagne goes with everything."

"We'll stick to that," he said.

"You mentioned it was a long day," Alana said, topping up his glass.

"Yes," Davey said. "After the conference tomorrow, it's just twenty-four hours until the weekend. I can't wait. I'll take my sons rugby training, then I'll be doing some serious running to limber up for the Iron Man. Another American invention."

"Whereas rugby is a fiendishly complicated British gift to the world," Alana said. "Davey, after three years in London, I've got my head round soccer, but rugby defeats me."

"Oh? Which soccer team do you favour?" Davey asked, somewhat sceptically.

"I'm rather fond of Crystal Palace," Alana replied. "It's great to see them holding their own in the Premier League."

Davey, who had spent his formative years not far from Selhurst Park, was astonished. "They're my favourite team," he said. "I watch them whenever I can. As a matter of fact, I nearly bought a house next door to Andy Johnson a few years ago." Laura had quashed that idea, he recalled with disappointment.

As he spoke about childhood heroes and the state of the current team, he was pleasantly surprised by Alana's knowledge of football and Crystal Palace in particular. Conversation flowed easily, as did the second bottle of champagne.

Predictably, Alana declined pudding, leaving Davey to tackle a deconstructed tiramisu alone. She ignored the sweets that were brought with their coffees. As Davey sipped his latte, Alana reached across the table for his hand. "I love London," she said, "but it's a lonely place. And so isolated at the top. Don't you feel it too, Davey?"

Her action was so unexpected that he didn't struggle, but she swiftly withdrew her hand anyway.

"There's a connection between us," Alana announced. "I can be myself with you. If I want to listen to Slayer instead of this goddamn jazz they're playing here, I know you won't judge me for it."

Davey was almost rendered speechless. Again, he would never have taken Alana for a kindred spirit, yet it seemed she shared his guilty pleasure. As a teenager, he'd loved heavy metal. He occasionally listened to it on his daily commute, although Laura thought Classic FM was more suitable for his station in life, and his car radio was tuned into it to humour her. "Did you say Slayer?" he asked Alana. "The metal band?"

"The very same," Alana said. "I listen to them each morning to start the day with energy. My iPhone's loaded with every track they ever laid down. Look, I'll prove it." She grabbed the phone from her valise.

Davey scanned the buzzing restaurant. "Maybe not here," he said.

"As it happens, they have a few rooms here, and I've booked one," Alana said. "I'm so bored with seeing all the London insurance faces at the Hyatt. I just wanted to be in a place where I didn't need to pretend. Come on up with me. We can get more coffees, listen to music." She patted her phone.

Relaxed after more than his fair share of champagne, Davey was tempted. He could have another coffee with Alana and take a cab back to the Hyatt. "All right," he said.

Alana asked for the bill to be charged to her room and ordered more coffee to be brought there.

Davey glanced around the reception lobby as she collected her key. He was sober enough to be concerned that no one he knew would see him. However innocent his intentions, they'd be easily misinterpreted. He didn't relish explaining to Laura why he'd been alone in a hotel bedroom with an attractive young woman, even if she was the insurance CEO who had fired him the year before.

Alana's room was painted in neutral shades of caramel and cream, not dissimilar to most of the business hotels where Davey stayed. A tray of coffee was already waiting for them.

Alana ignored it, taking a Bose Bluetooth speaker from her valise. She pressed a few buttons, and the unmistakable sound of heavy metal filled the room. "Do you believe me now?" she asked, flicking back her sleek bob.

"Yes," Davey said. He shook his head rhythmically backwards and forwards. "This was better when I had hair," he admitted ruefully.

"Like this?" Alana asked, copying his motion. Her bob swung across her face.

"You've got it." Davey found he was grinning like a madman.

Alana sat on the bed, stretching her long, slender legs. Her skin, the colour of the tiny espressos she drank, had a silken sheen. Caught up in the heat of corporate deals and the upheaval of his exit from Veritable, he'd never appreciated before how alluring she was. He felt the heat rise in his groin.

Alana reached for his hand again. Davey let her take it. He ignored the rational mind that told him infidelity was wrong, that Laura deserved better. She would never know. He didn't resist when Alana brushed her lips against his, or when she kissed with more passion, her tongue probing and licking the tip of his. He gently pushed back, tasting the coffee on her breath.

Alana seemed to be enjoying herself. She placed Davey's left hand on her leg, letting him feel her smooth skin, then guided his fingers to the inside of her thigh and up to her lacy panties.

"It's getting a little hot in here," she said. Drawing back from him, she unzipped her dress, letting it fall to the ground. Skimpy, bright red underwear contrasted with her dark, toned body. Her brown eyes shone.

Davey told himself he'd be crazy to refuse her. He leaned forward, kissing Alana's lips, neck and shoulders, while unclipping her bra strap. "You're beautiful," he murmured.

"And you're so fit," Alana said. "When I saw you this morning in your shorts, I was blown away by those muscles." She loosened his shirt, biting his neck, nipping at his nipples and hairy chest, then unbuckling his belt, kneeling and nibbling his thighs.

"I want to go further than this," she said, suddenly producing a condom from her valise.

"What are you doing?" Davey asked, smelling the scent of chocolate as she unwrapped it.

"Trust me," Alana said. "It'll be great."

She put the condom on him and applied her mouth to his groin.

The sensation as she moved her lips and tongue over him was almost too exquisite. "Alana," Davey groaned, shuddering. He began to thrust towards her throat, almost caught unawares as a rush of hot liquid arrived without warning.

He felt obliged to apologise. His performance left much to be desired. "I'm sorry," he began.

Alana put a finger to her lips. "There's no need to be. The night is young," she said, cupping his hands around her breasts. Stroking Davey's bottom and thighs, she nibbled his nipples again while he squeezed hers.

"Oh God. Alana." He moaned her name, over and over again.

"You're a fit guy," Alana said. "Well, I bet you can last for hours."

She slipped off her panties, encouraging Davey to fling his clothes on the floor while she retrieved another condom from her bag. Gently, almost with reverence, she stroked the sheath onto him.

He entered her, the excitement nearly too much to bear. Alana mirrored it. She sighed with delight, writhing beneath him as he pounded steadily.

"You like that, don't you?" Davey murmured.

"Yes," she said, her voice husky.

He did his best to compensate for his earlier gaffe, taking Alana to the brink of ecstasy and then, tantalisingly, withdrawing. All the while, he kissed and caressed her. Her iPhone played Slayer noisily in the background.

Alana surrendered to him completely, squealing as he teased her, clasping him closer to draw him back within. Eventually, her arousal was complete. As she gasped and moaned, wriggling beneath him, Davey finally reached a climax too.

"That was awesome," Alana said.

"I know." Davey smirked. "I've always wanted to make love to Slayer."

Chapter 6 **Marty**

It was twenty four hours before Erik returned Marty's call. Meanwhile, Marty considered asking Amy to sound out his partner on the possibility of selling darria tea and developing a prescription drug in parallel. He forbore from contacting her, in the end. She'd made it clear she didn't want to be involved in the dispute.

While he was impressed by her market research, he wasn't going to tell her. She'd only ask for a pay rise, or pester him again for a transfer to his vodka business. It was a magnet for young people, who believed marketing a high end vodka meant an endless round of promotional parties and visits to clubs. Every year, he received dozens of unsolicited job applications from marketing graduates like Amy. He conceded she knew her stuff, though. His elder daughter currently managed the Snow Mountain brand for him. If she tired of it, or decided to start a family, he could always call on Amy. She was a safety net, at least.

Erik phoned when Marty was meeting his bank manager. Seeing the number, Marty immediately excused himself and stepped outside.

"Did you get my message?" he asked Erik.

"Of course," Erik replied. "We need to talk."

"Let's do that over a pint," Marty suggested.

He drove to the Jewellery Quarter. Parking nearby, he walked through the winding cobbled passage where the old workshop was located. The property was unrecognisable from the shabby building he'd bought at auction. On the ground floor, there was now an open plan office, its brick walls painted white and its salvaged oak floor varnished. Aluminium pipes carried utilities across the ceiling and down the walls. The lighting was industrial-chic, the air scented with the aroma of a coffee machine in a dining area at the back. Four young people sat in front of laptops at pale wood desks: Erik, Amy and a couple of web developers who also rented flats in the building.

Amy glanced up at him, her eyes pleading. Marty dismissed her concerns with a wave of his hand. "Ready, Erik?" he said. "I don't want the pub to sell out."

Marty gave him the news as soon as he'd bought beer. "I'm going to fund research trials," he said. "However much it costs, I'm in for it. And..."

"...we'll be selling tea to pay for it," Erik said.

Marty feigned astonishment. "You took the words from my mouth."

"I've been talking to Amy," Erik said. "She's explained that the tea will fund the research. It could work. We need to source enough darria, that's all. That will take time."

"No, it won't," Marty said. "You told me it grows like a weed in the mountain valleys of Bazakistan. So, I'll go there, buy up land, establish a plantation, and in two years we'll have a harvest." Land and labour were both cheap in Bazakistan. His plan was faultless.

Erik had a different opinion. "Bazakistan is too dangerous," he said solemnly.

"I've been doing business there for over twenty years," Marty pointed out. "Look. Not a scratch on me."

"You haven't offended anyone important," Erik said. "Yet. Don't forget how we first met, and what happened afterwards. My father might have owned a vodka factory, but that didn't save him when he annoyed a petty official. He ended up dead." He looked away, shuddering. "My sister and I would have been killed too, if we hadn't been studying in the UK."

"It was a huge shock to me when your father was arrested," Marty said. "I paid his legal bill, and your sister's school fees, come to that. I did what I could to help."

"Kat doesn't think so," Erik said. He swigged beer, emptying his glass.

Silence hung like a curtain between them. After a while, Erik added, "I'm not saying I agree with my sister. But Bazakistan brings challenges we shouldn't take lightly. Even if you're friendly with the old régime, don't imagine it will be in place forever. Your business partners almost certainly haven't mentioned that young people in Bazakistan are increasingly becoming radicalised. Fundamentalist preachers are stirring up trouble among some of the Muslim youths, but mostly, my countrymen simply harbour grudges. The President has allowed his buddies to grab land for building developments and minerals extraction. Bazaki clans have long memories."

Marty was sceptical. "I've told you before, Erik. I've seen nothing of this on my visits to Bazakistan. Harry Aliyev is completely relaxed about the political situation."

Erik's eyes narrowed at the mention of the man who'd supplanted his father at the Snow Mountain distillery. "He wouldn't want you to find out," Erik said. "Why would he frighten you away, and risk his little goldmine? He's lucky the British media isn't interested in a country far away. But it's the talk of the Bazaki expatriate community back here, especially the political exiles. Ken Khan is the name on everyone's lips as the likely leader of the revolution. He's clever, a graduate who's served in the Army and made good connections in it, and he's got the students on his side. His wife's in London. She slipped out of Bazakistan through the mountains when she heard the security services were after her. We both know they wouldn't be gentle."

"I'll get you another beer," Marty said, hoping to divert Erik's thoughts from the horrors of the past. The younger man needed to relax.

He reflected as the pints were pulled. Erik's view of Bazakistan was at odds with his, for understandable reasons. Marty was merely an occasional visitor to the country, appreciated by the government and his business contacts for the foreign currency he brought them. Even if Erik was right about the risk of revolution, there was no reason why a new government wouldn't be sympathetic to him too. Whoever was in power, they'd welcome another venture that brought them plenty of sterling – and dollars, euros and more, if darria was as big as he expected it to be.

"You'll have to trust me on this, Erik," he said, placing their pints on the table. "This drug has a bright future. The sooner we can commercialise it, the better. So I want to grow plenty of darria and launch the tea at the earliest opportunity."

"Yes, but we shouldn't grow it in Bazakistan," Erik said. "I've been telling you we should be able to replicate ideal conditions for darria elsewhere. All we need do in Bazakistan is test the climate and soil conditions, then seek a more stable country in which to cultivate it."

"That'll take too long," Marty said, reasonably, in his view.

Erik rolled his eyes in frustration. "It's unwise to put all our eggs in one basket. We should be looking for supplies from multiple sources, not just one."

He had a point. "Okay," Marty said. "We can do all that, and diversify our supply chain, while the first crop is growing in Bazakistan. We need to start there, because darria cultivation is totally untested anywhere else."

"You're too impatient," Erik said. "I can see I won't persuade you. But, as you British like to say, it's your funeral."

He spoke in the plummy tones of his English boarding school. Marty had to bite his tongue to avoid sniggering. He realised Erik's fears were no laughing matter, albeit he didn't concur with them.

Darria wasn't Marty's only concern when he thought of Bazakistan. His conversation with Charles was nagging him. "Erik," he said, "Am I right? Amy's father works with your sister's fiancé, doesn't he?"

"Yes," Erik replied. He looked puzzled.

"It's beginning to make sense," Marty said. "Her father said a colleague was planning a business trip to Bazakistan. I'm guessing that business isn't insurance. Kat thinks the Snow Mountain factory is rightfully hers."

Erik said nothing.

"Just suppose," Marty said carefully, "that her boyfriend's going to Bazakistan to try to get it back for her? Or worse still, she's travelling there herself?"

Erik jumped to his feet. "She's crazy! She'll be killed."

"You'd better tell her," Marty said.

Chapter 7 **Davey**

She didn't call. He'd said to her he'd never done this before, and she'd laughed merrily and said she hoped they'd do it again soon, many times.

He'd left her room, then, and taken a cab back to the Hyatt. He'd only seen her from afar the next day, networking with others, or standing on the podium while her audience hung on her every word. Then he'd returned to London, to another day at the office and the longed-for weekend that somehow had lost its sparkle.

After a week, he called her. "Alana? It's me."

"Davey?" That same throaty laugh. "When can we see each other?"

"How about tonight?" he said.

"Sorry, I'm busy." She suggested a date another week hence.

He took her address and made excuses to his wife about working late next week. He stopped asking Laura for sex. She didn't remind him. He imagined she was wrapped up in the children.

At the appointed hour, he buzzed Alana's doorbell. She lived in the City, near Moorgate and the old offices that Bishopstoke had occupied before they took over the Veritable building by the Thames. Alana had his old view of the river, his former PA, his former friends. Once you were over the hill, when redundancy hit you like an express train, you found out who your real friends were.

He hadn't realised Alana was one of them.

She greeted him as if it were he who'd made her wait. "I've missed you so much," she breathed. "Here, fix us both a bourbon, and let's chill. I'll put music on." She handed him a bottle and two crystal tumblers.

The bourbon was aged and smooth, another American triumph. They clinked glasses. Slayer was playing, louder this time. "My apartment's soundproofed," she said.

Davey suspected if anyone banged on the door to complain, he wouldn't hear them. Alana had a top of the range Sonos soundbar, and knew how to use it. "Nice place," he said, looking around as he sipped his drink. From the floor to ceiling window, he spotted the plush office building that housed the Association of British Insurers. It reminded him that the heart of his industry lay in the tall glass buildings rising from this web of medieval streets. "I'm afraid I can't always meet you here," he said anxiously. "I might bump into someone I know."

Alana didn't attempt to disagree. "Rent a pied-à-terre," she said.

Her sitting room was dark red, like a womb. Her sofa was velvet, yielding as she pulled him onto it.

Davey kissed her, pressing his tongue against hers, enjoying the sweet whiskey on her breath. He began to unzip her dress.

"Not yet," Alana said.

"Oh?" he queried. "Don't you want me?"

"More than ever," she murmured. "Longer and longer." She reached for a gold pillbox on the coffee table in front of them and emptied its contents on a red lacquered tray. "Magic dust," she said, sweeping the snow-white powder into two lines, holding her nose to one of them and drawing in the particles.

She offered him the tray. "Why not?" he said, a naughty schoolboy grin on his face. As the rush hit him, he knew he was man enough for anyone – especially his demanding, inexhaustible lover, who was drawing him towards her at last.

Chapter 8 **Kat**

Of all her fiancé's friends, Kat had warmed the most towards Ted Edwards. If she'd stopped to consider it, she would probably have labelled the feeling as gratitude. Strapped for cash in the days before she met Ross, Kat had been persuaded to marry four illegal immigrants for money. Ted had worked hard to convince the authorities to drop all charges against her.

His solicitor's practice was based in Lincoln's Inn Fields, the elegant Georgian garden square behind Holborn station. Although a prestigious address, his premises were poky, sloping-ceilinged rooms at the top of a five storey building with no lift. Kat almost regretted donning her new Louboutins by the time she'd climbed several flights of stairs.

Ted, tall, stocky, and untidy, seemed to occupy most of the small library in which he conducted meetings. He sprawled in his moulded plastic chair, a sandy thatch of hair flopping into his brown eyes. "Feel free to smoke," he told her, with what might have been a conspiratorial wink, "as long as you don't set fire to my law books. Strictly, it's illegal to light up, but I won't tell if you won't."

Kat was smug. "I've given up." It was mostly true. She occasionally smoked a Silk Cut Ultra to enjoy a subtle hint of her old habit, but Ross and his friends didn't need to know.

"Ross must be a good influence," Ted said. "Fancy that."

He offered coffee from a Nespresso machine, following her eyes as they rested on the room's cobwebbed crannies. "You were expecting luxury," he said.

Kat laughed lightly. "You're right," she admitted.

"I don't aim to impress with swish offices," Ted said. "My reputation is all I need. Friends and clients know I deliver. I'm more likely to travel to meetings – in police stations, for example. Talking of which, you relinquished your passport to the police last year. I've got it back." He handed it over.

Kat took it reverentially, as if it were made of gold. The burgundy document was her most prized possession. With it, she was free to travel anywhere: across the world, even in and out of Bazakistan. For this, and only this, she was grateful to Marty Bridges. He had helped her acquire a British passport when she was a schoolchild in the UK, suddenly homeless and friendless following her father's arrest. "Thank you," she said to Ted. "Is that the end of the matter?"

"Almost," Ted said. "The police have confirmed they'll take no further action. I must confess, when Ross first asked me to act as your solicitor, I didn't rate your chances. But your version of events has been accepted. The Crown acknowledges that when you married illegal immigrants, you were acting under duress. They haven't found any witnesses who'd say otherwise."

Kat was hardly surprised by his last comment. She suspected potential witnesses were either dead or had made themselves scarce. "I'm glad it's over," she said. "I'm not proud of what happened. I want to make a new life with Ross and move forward."

"Ah, yes. Congratulations on your engagement," Ted said. "That brings me to the small problem that's still outstanding. Although you used false identities to marry the four foreign gentlemen, I'm afraid you remain legally married to the first of them."

"But I was put under pressure," Kat said, allowing her lip to tremble. She admitted to herself, if not Ted, that the only pressure she'd been under was financial.

"Not to worry," Ted said, stretching his legs even more. "I'll get it annulled for you. Can I assume I'll be invited to your next wedding?"

"The minute we've set a date," Kat assured him. Ross would insist Ted was there. As old schoolfriends, they'd probably go on a stag weekend together, too.

"I'll get cracking on that annulment, then," Ted said. "As soon as it's done, you can plan your nuptials with Ross." He beamed brightly, revealing unexpectedly even, dazzling white teeth.

Kat recalled a childhood trip to an aquarium famous for its tunnel of sharks. It was the pièce de résistance, a corridor with a giant fish tank wrapped around it and a gift shop at the other end. She'd looked a shark in the eye, shivering at its alien intelligence and hunger, glad a glass wall stood between them. Ted's eyes, brown and beady, fixed onto hers now. She was relieved they were on the same side.

"Glad it's in progress," she said, steering their discussion towards business. "We arranged the meeting to discuss Snow Mountain vodka. How can I recover my father's assets?"

"A lot depends on the Bazaki legal system," Ted said. "It's not my speciality, so I've arranged for a Bazaki lawyer to join us. He'll be here

44

in ten minutes. Meanwhile, why don't you tell me more about Snow Mountain? Until Ross approached me about this project, I just knew it as an exclusive vodka brand. Men order it to impress the girls in some of London's nicer clubs. I'd like to know more of its history."

"Bazakistan was part of the USSR," Kat began. "My father, Sasha Belov, was an engineer. He managed a vodka factory in Kireniat. That's the second largest city in Bazakistan."

Ted nodded. "So he bought the factory when Bazakistan became independent of the Soviet Union?"

"That's right," Kat said. "In 1991."

"I know Russian oligarchs acquired assets at a knockdown price around that time," Ted began.

Kat interrupted him. "My father was hardly an oligarch," she said. "The factory was all he had. We're not Russian either, we're Bazaki. I mean, my parents were originally from Russia, but they lived in Bazakistan for most of their lives." She stopped abruptly. Those lives had been brutally cut short. She would have to tell him all about that, refreshing her memories, reopening her wounds.

"Do you know how he paid for the factory?" Ted asked. "It might have been a bank loan, or perhaps there was another shareholder, a sleeping partner who contributed the cash."

"I don't know," Kat said. "I'm not even sure how much it cost. I was a toddler at the time." A blurry recollection surfaced: of a younger, thinner Marty Bridges arriving on a motorbike, handing over a briefcase stuffed with banknotes. She shook her head. "What I do know," she said, "is that he made a big success of developing Snow Mountain as a new premium brand. His commitment to quality was second to none. He also took an early decision to concentrate on exporting to the West, and that's where Marty Bridges came on the scene."

"Who's he?" Ted asked.

"Our distributor," Kat said. "He's based here in England, but he sells Snow Mountain worldwide. For some reason, my father wouldn't work with anyone else. Bridges has made a small fortune out of it." Her lips tightened.

"That's very helpful," Ted said. "I know it will be painful for you, Kat – Ross has told me a little of the background – but would you mind filling me in on the circumstances that led to your father losing control of Snow Mountain, please?"

Kat took a deep breath. "Eleven years ago, my father was thrown into prison," she said. "He'd done nothing wrong. My mother wrote to me – I was only fourteen, and at boarding school in England – to say she was sure his name would be cleared and he'd be free soon. But he wasn't."

Ted's eyes widened sympathetically. "I assume Bazakistan is the sort of place where you can be arrested for dropping litter."

"Yes, it's a police state," Kat said. "Usually, you just bribe them and they let you out."

"But that didn't happen," Ted mused. "Any idea why not?"

"He can't have bribed the right people," Kat said, "or paid them enough. Marty could have helped him out. He'd made enough money out of my father, after all. Instead, he couldn't wait to do business with Arystan Aliyev." She virtually spat out his name. "That's the crook who ended up with the factory. The state confiscated it and gave it to him. Then my father died at the hands of a firing squad."

Ted immediately passed her a tissue. Kat took it gratefully and dabbed at her eyes.

"What about the rest of your family?" Ted asked.

"Letters from my mother stopped when my father died," Kat said. "I couldn't get in touch with her, however hard I tried." Although desperately short of money, she'd spent her limited resources on phone calls, and even a private investigator. She'd drawn a blank. Maria Belova had disappeared without trace. "They must have killed her too."

"That's terrible," Ted said. He patted her hand. "I can't bring your parents back – if only I could – but rest assured, I'll do whatever I can to recover that vodka factory. The key questions to address are whether your father owned it and whether it was illegally seized. That's why Arman Khan's visiting my office in a moment. He's a bright young lad."

He had a soothing manner, and Kat regretted comparing him with a shark. She composed herself sufficiently to smile brightly when Arman Khan arrived.

He was perhaps in his late twenties, a few years younger than Ted, with the olive skin and heavy features of an ethnic Bazaki. His sleek black hair and trim beard framed an intense expression. Nearly as tall as Ted, he suddenly made the library seem even more claustrophobic.

Ted noticed. "Why don't I brief Arman on your situation, then we can grab a latte round the corner?" He summarised Kat's story, finishing by asking Arman how Kat could regain control of the factory and brand rights.

Arman fixed his intense gaze on Kat. The image of the fish tank returned, and it was with some effort that she stopped herself flinching.

"I don't think the English courts can help you," Arman said, his voice soft with barely a hint of an accent. "Bazaki law applies to Bazaki assets. We need to be clear what the assets are, of course. With the limited information Ted gave me before, I took the liberty of having the Kireniat commercial registers checked. The Snow Mountain Company, first incorporated in Kireniat in 1992, owns land on the edge of the city and the local trademark registration for Snow Mountain."

"Who owns the Snow Mountain Company?" Ted asked.

"I'm waiting to find out," Arman replied.

"Let's assume it's Mr Aliyev," Ted said. "In that case, what can Kat do to regain ownership of the company for her family?"

Arman addressed Kat. "The shares should have passed to you on the death of your parents," he said. "You're an only child, I guess?"

Kat pursed her lips. "I have a brother," she said, "but he's not interested in vodka."

"Unusual for a young man," Ted observed.

That was typical of the rather dry sense of humour displayed by Ross and his friends. Kat waited a second or so before saying more. "I meant in the professional sense," she told Ted, adding, "Erik's always been more of a gardener." Give her brother a square inch of soil, and he'd find a way to grow a beautiful flower on it. On the other hand, Kat, taken daily into the distillery as a small child, had grown to love the hustle and bustle of the factory, the tanks and pipes twisting like a Heath Robinson drawing, the rows of bottles full of crystalline spirit. It was understood within the family that she'd be schooled in England to learn the international language of commerce, then work for Marty with the aim of taking over the distribution of the product in due course.

"The good news is that Bazakistan has equal rights for women," Arman said. "A Communist legacy. So you have equal inheritance rights with your brother, Kat. The bad news is that he's in line for fifty per cent of your parents' estate, so you'll need his co-operation."

"I presume we don't just write to the commercial registry in Bazakistan and say Kat wants to claim her inheritance?" Ted asked.

"Not quite," Arman said. "There are forms to be completed, court proceedings to be taken, commissions to be paid."

"Bribes?" Ted asked.

"Commissions," Arman repeated.

"I take it you can organise all this from London?" Ted said.

Arman tutted. "Not really. You'll have to go to Bazakistan, Kat, and lodge the claim in person."

Kat felt dizzy. She hadn't expected that. Glancing at Ted for support, she noted he seemed concerned too.

"This is a country where the authorities killed Kat's parents," Ted said gently.

Arman smiled. "You really needn't worry, Kat. Bazakistan's changed a lot in eleven years. It's had to modernise rapidly since independence. I'm sure commissions to the right people can fix any legal problems."

"How civilised, and how unlike the UK," Ted murmured. "What sort of money are we talking about?"

"Up to a hundred thousand," Arman said casually. "That's dollars, not sterling, of course. I'll need twenty thou upfront to put a couple of people on retainer."

"I'll have to discuss it with my client, naturally," Ted said. "What we really need to know is the likelihood of success. Mr Aliyev must be a rich man and would surely put up a fight."

"I would argue that Mr Aliyev didn't acquire the factory lawfully," Arman said. "I believe the chances are good. Whatever Mr Belov did, the seizure of his property was disproportionate."

"He was innocent," Kat said.

Ted nodded. "I know, Kat, and that should further improve your chances. It sounds like you can get what you want. I suggest Ross goes to Bazakistan with you, and if I know Ross, he'll want to anyway. Let's repair to the coffee shop on the corner and discuss timings and travel plans."

Kat glanced uneasily at their eager faces. She should be excited at advancing towards her goal, but she couldn't dispel a deep sense of foreboding.

Chapter 9 **Davey**

When Davey Saxton was CEO of Veritable, his nearest and dearest received thoughtfully chosen gifts and cards on special occasions. They were selected with great care by his efficient personal assistant. Life at Saxton Brown was different. Davey shared a PA with the rest of his team. The flowers he bought to celebrate his nephew's birth were purchased in a hurry at Liverpool Street station. He jumped on the tube, leaving it at Great Portland Street and jogging for ten minutes through Regents Park before arriving at Dee's Georgian semi in Primrose Hill.

Dee earned so much from her online wellness activities that she could comfortably afford a full-time housekeeper and two nannies. A day after George's birth, she looked relaxed and refreshed. Her spacious house was tidy, newly decorated in light, airy shades of blue, grey and off-white. A Mercedes sat on the drive. The front room resembled a hothouse. At least a dozen bouquets had preceded Davey's bunch of lilies. Dee was still able to find a vase for them.

They hugged. "How are you?" he asked.

"Fine," she said. "Would you like to see him? He's asleep."

George lay swaddled in a Moses basket: a cute, red-faced scrap with a shock of dark hair. A tiny cotton hat made him look even more pixie-ish.

"He's got your nose," Davey said, without much conviction.

The baby's eyes rolled beneath their lids. "He's dreaming," Dee said. "So far, he's been very calm."

"Meditating already," Davey said. "How did the birth go?" He rather dreaded the answer, but he knew Laura would want a blow by blow account.

"Four hours, without painkillers. Thank goodness for yoga," Dee said.

Davey quizzed her at length about the journey to hospital, her short stay there, the medics in attendance, the baby's weight, height and his full name. Charles, contacted at work, had arrived two hours before the birth.

Davey recalled Charles' abrupt, almost panicked, departure from the office. "I thought you weren't going to tell him about the birth," he said. "You swore me to secrecy. That was awkward." Although Davey tried to keep his relations with colleagues on a professional footing and wouldn't have volunteered information about Dee in any event, Charles had tried to press him for it. "Only last week, he asked me outright if you were expecting a baby. I told him he should ask you." Davey had known that would be a waste of time; Dee wasn't responding to Charles' emails and phone calls, and she'd moved out of her Mayfair flat without giving him her new address.

"Sorry," Dee said. "I changed my mind. I thought he should know after all. Whatever he's done, it would be wrong to deny him the experience of being present at the birth."

"Was he excited?" Davey asked, secretly relieved not to have received an invitation himself.

"He was nervous. As soon as he'd given George a quick cuddle, he hared outside for a smoke." She winced. "I wish he hadn't. It was a cigar. You could tell from the stink on his clothes when he reappeared."

"You used to smoke yourself," Davey pointed out.

"Not cigars," Dee said. "It's a taste I've never wished to acquire. I just about tolerated his cigarette habit when Charles and I were together."

She'd once admitted to Davey that she began smoking as a teenager to win her way into Charles' affections. Charles was the coolest guy they knew then, a few years older than Davey, and hero of the school football team. Dee hadn't been the only girl pursuing him. Sporty, scruffy and chubby, she didn't stand a chance.

Although they'd played football together at school, Davey had forgotten all about Charles once they left. Dee hadn't. Two years ago, she'd announced without warning that Charles had moved in with her. Eighteen months later and equally suddenly, just as Davey had given Charles a job, it became clear that Dee was pregnant and Charles had left her.

Davey studied his sister's appearance: her creamy skin, golden hair, and slim figure that appeared almost untouched by pregnancy. The chunky teenager was gone. She and Charles had been a good-looking couple.

It was a shame they were no longer together. Children needed a father around. Besides, whatever had passed between Charles and Dee, Davey liked his IT director. Charles was good company, and straightforward. His IT skills were fundamental to Saxton Brown's success. Davey suspected the relationship with Dee would have lasted longer if it hadn't started so soon after Charles' divorce.

"Are you planning to see much of Charles?" he asked.

"I won't stop him seeing his son," Dee said. "I'll have nothing to do with him otherwise. My teenage infatuation twenty-five years ago was no basis for a relationship now. I was crazy to think any different."

She was protesting too much, Davey thought. If Charles hadn't walked out, Dee would still be praising him to the skies. She'd virtually thrown herself at the man two years before, having met him in a nightclub and discovered he was newly single.

George awoke, looking around solemnly with huge blue eyes. Dee decided they should take him into the garden. She wrapped the little boy in a blanket.

They walked down a staircase to the basement, a stainless steel kitchen with a large dining area and French doors at the rear. Dee's house was larger at the back than the front: four storeys instead of three. The property was a step up in size from her old flat.

It was a fine spring evening, sunny, and as warm as the season allowed. A lilac tree threw its heady scent over the long, narrow plot. Dee showed him how she'd left old trees in situ, for fruit and climbing, while designing a garden suitable for a small child. There was a lawn, a play area and a herb patch. Furthest from the house, a locked gate led to a mooring on the Regents Canal. One day, she would build a boathouse, Dee said. She and George would speed across London by water, ignoring the traffic-choked streets.

They sat on hammocks under the lilac tree. Davey stroked George's soft hair. Dee told him how glad she was that the decorators had just finished. It had been touch and go whether renovations would be completed in time for the baby's arrival.

"I'm sending the builders round to the flat in Mayfair now," Dee said. "I'll be renting it to an oligarch, so I'm making it perfect to attract the best tenant."

Davey assumed that would be the tenant who paid the most money. "Are you sure it needs work?" he asked doubtfully. The flat was already finished to a high specification in the cool greys that Dee favoured, ornate mirrors and chandeliers adding a touch of bling.

"More than you'd think," Dee said. "The paintwork needs freshening. Little scuffs, the sort you and I would overlook, mean hundreds off the rent. They'll expect power showers. Then there's the balcony floor. It's rotten, and has to be replaced."

"How long will that take?" he asked.

"A couple of months," Dee said, "if the time the decorators spent here is any guide."

Alana had suggested he rented a pied-à-terre. Another option suddenly presented itself. "Could I stay there occasionally until you rent it out? I'm always working late at the office these days. Staying over in central London would help me keep my exercise programme and sleep on track. Commuting is just dead time."

Dee looked at him sharply. Had she realised he was having an affair? His pulse quickened, imagining Dee telling Laura; then tears, recriminations and divorce. On Saturday mornings, he would join the sad dads he saw at rugby training, gazing wistfully at the children they would hand back at teatime.

"I don't understand," Dee said. "You've worked in the City for years without buying into that macho long hours culture. Why now?"

"We're a start-up," Davey said, as if that explained everything. He grinned with relief. She suspected nothing.

"Well, don't forget your mindfulness techniques," Dee said. "Even two minutes of meditation is as good as an hour's sleep. You're welcome to use the flat. It's not fully furnished, though. I only left a few pieces to display the flat to prospective tenants. It has to be properly dressed. If there's anything you need, let me know and I'll have it sent round."

"Thanks," Davey said. All he needed was a bed.

They returned to the kitchen so she could fetch keys. He noted the calendar hanging on the wall. It was refreshingly free of appointments.

"Are you taking it easy for a month or so?" Davey asked.

"Of course," Dee said. "I've told my clients I'm spending time getting to know George. I can afford it. My online videos are making money while I sleep. I've made sure not to take on new clients lately. The last one was an insurance highflyer, actually."

"Really?" Davey said. "Anyone I know?"

"Alana Green," Dee replied. "She said she'd met you."

Picturing his lover's naked body, Davey suppressed a leer. "I hardly know her," he lied.

"Yes, I worked that out. She was fascinated by you, I think," Dee said. "She bombarded me with questions about you. I ended up telling her about your mediocre football team, the Iron Man, your ridiculous taste in music. She hung on my every word. And do you know the very strangest thing?"

52

"You must tell me," Davey said weakly, stunned by the revelations but flattered that Alana had been so keen to pursue him.

"Alana didn't even have time to meditate. She had to dash back to her office. Her secretary cancelled all the other meetings she'd put in my diary." Dee shook her head in disapproval. "That woman doesn't know how to relax."

Chapter 10 **Kat**

"What do you mean, we're not going to Bazakistan?" Kat said. "I don't understand." It was in the middle of the afternoon, and she was packing a suitcase for the next day. Their tickets, passports and currency were safe in a travel wallet. A cab was booked to take them to Heathrow in the morning.

"I'm sorry, darling," Ross said, his voice gruff. Theatrically, he put a hand to his brow. "I've got a hellish headache, my throat feels as if I've swallowed a box of drawing pins, and my temperature's way above normal." He flopped onto their bed. "I just want to sleep. I saw the GP as an emergency case. He says it's flu and I need to rest, not travel."

"You can rest on the plane," Kat said, perturbed.

"No way would I disobey doctor's orders," Ross said. "I'm afraid the trip's off, darling."

He looked dreadful, his skin waxy and beaded with sweat. Of course he shouldn't travel. But where did that leave her? Arman Khan had arranged a court hearing, and she couldn't afford to miss it.

"Okay," Kat said. "I can see why you shouldn't go to Bazakistan, but there's nothing preventing me." She tried to hide her fear. It mustn't stop her now, not when she was so close to recovering her family business and her purpose in life.

Ross looked concerned. "Erik felt it was too dangerous for you to travel alone," he said. "In fact, he didn't want you to go at all."

"Erik's an old woman. He thought it was too dangerous, full stop," Kat pointed out. "That's not what the lawyers are saying. Money talks in Bazakistan." At last, thanks to Ross, she was in a position to have her say.

"I'd trust Ted's judgement, but the lawyers are just some Bazaki guys he knows, aren't they?" Ross said. "If I were them, I'd pretend Bazakistan was an earthly paradise to keep the fees rolling in. Anyway, I'm starting to think this factory is too much of a distraction. You won't have time to run it, once we're married with a baby or two. You do want children, don't you? Everyone I know seems to be having them, even Charles."

"Amy's father?" Kat was puzzled. "Surely not, at his age? Amy never mentioned anything."

"He's just become a father again," Ross said. "I'm actually rather jealous. A child is the only legacy we truly leave behind on this earth. Our genes will live forever, whereas a factory will crumble to dust. It's only bricks and mortar, after all."

Ross wasn't usually philosophical. "You've definitely got a fever," Kat said impatiently. "Try to sleep, and let me finish packing." She ignored the twinge of guilt that suggested Ross needed her by his side. He'd be over his flu within days, whereas she only had one chance to recover Snow Mountain and show the world what she could do with it.

Ross groaned. "Please don't go."

"If you really cared, you'd let me." Kat looked soulfully into his eyes. That always won him over.

Chapter 11 **Marty**

Bazakair shared its Heathrow business lounge with a number of other airlines. Bored with the grainy photographs of models in The Sun, Marty tried to guess where the other passengers were flying. He was sure the rowdy group of young men in the corner were the Bazaki national football team. They stayed put as flights were called for Karachi, Kuala Lumpur and Canberra. He was about to help himself to more complimentary beer when he saw Kat.

She strode into the lounge, long blonde locks swinging above a pale cashmere coat. It had been a year since they last met, a fortunately brief occasion when they'd exchanged harsh words across Erik's hospital bed. Erik was fine now. Marty and Kat's regard for each other was anything but. Marty wondered whether to ignore or acknowledge her.

He chose the latter, standing in her path and offering a handshake. "How's tricks, young Kat?"

She looked at him with unconcealed dislike, although her warm, smooth hand took his for a second or two. "To what do I owe this unexpected pleasure?" she asked.

"I'm visiting the distillery," Marty said. He was actually planning to view a few parcels of land, and had been in two minds whether to see Harry at the vodka factory at all. "How about you?"

"Oh, things to do, people to see," she said. "I've spotted someone I know. Must go – Ciao."

Marty doubted she knew the Bazaki footballers, but from their leers and frenzied waving, it was clear they wanted to put that right. She sauntered over to them and began a conversation in Russian. Marty didn't bother to listen.

The flight to Bazaku City and Kireniat was called. Marty was unamused to find his suspicions were correct. Kat, too, was travelling to Bazakistan. She donned her cashmere coat again and strode out of the lounge, admiring footballers clustered around her.

Marty followed them, certain now that he should meet Harry in Kireniat. Kat didn't look in his direction again until, boarding the aircraft, she glanced over her shoulder and whispered to the flight attendant. When he was seated, he wasn't surprised to see that she was as far away from him as the confines of the club class cabin allowed.

Marty set his watch to Bazaki time, early evening in Kireniat. Ordering plenty of red wine to compensate for Bazakair's poor beer selection, he settled in his seat to view the latest Bond movie.

Chapter 12 **Kat**

As the Airbus circled above Kireniat, Kat stared through the oval window. A lump rose in her throat at the familiar sight: lush farms around the city, newly clothed in spring green, and snow-tipped mountains beyond. Only Kireniat's skyline had changed in the last eleven years. There were taller, shinier buildings glittering in the morning sunlight.

She was both excited and apprehensive. This wasn't just her birthplace, it was the city whose officials had consigned her parents to an early death in gaol. To quell her lingering fears, she swigged from the small bottle of champagne provided by Bazakair for a Bucks Fizz breakfast. Some of the footballers noticed, and gave her the thumbs up. They passed pieces of paper to her with names and phone numbers hastily scribbled down. She smiled, withholding her own number. While their chat in the lounge at Heathrow had been fun, helping her relax, Kat didn't want it to go further.

Her spirits began to lift. Bazakistan was different now. Even the shape of the city below was evidence of that. She had money, thanks to Ross, and that made a difference. Kat had no illusions about the nature of commissions brokered by Arman Khan.

She waited until Marty Bridges, the football team, and the other club class passengers had disembarked. Strolling after them with her precious British passport, she was waved through immigration with barely a glance.

A handful of large Western hotel brands had arrived in Kireniat. Kat took a cab from the airport to the InterContinental, a showy skyscraper with a polished granite lobby and huge rooms. Although it was early, the receptionist booked her in immediately. Kat refreshed herself with a shower, ordered from room service, and asked the concierge to arrange a taxi to Arman's offices.

Unlike Ted, Arman invested in ostentation. His premises were on the eighth floor of a glitzy newbuild overlooking the former People's Palace, now City Hall. Kat was escorted to a meeting room by a young blonde secretary. Their heels click-clacked in unison across the marble floor. If anything, the girl's stilettos were even higher than Kat's.

Arman was sitting at a circular table, a view of downtown Kireniat behind him. He motioned to Kat to sit opposite. She saw that the black glass table was, in fact, made of many small tables, each shaped like a slice of cake.

The secretary served strong coffee in tiny white espresso cups, without being asked. Kat sipped hers gratefully.

"So," Arman said, gesturing expansively behind him, "What do you think of the new Kireniat?"

"I see a lot of change," she said. "I hope it's been enough to give me my factory back."

Arman leaned backwards. His chair, a chrome and leather Bauhaus copy, rocked, not quite tipping him out. "No problem," he said, grinning. "I've lodged your claim with the commercial court. They were supposed to discuss it tomorrow but it's been postponed until Friday. How long are you here?"

"I'd planned to fly back on Thursday," Kat said, "but I'll stay as long as it takes. Why the deferral – is it Aliyev's doing?"

"I don't think so, and I don't envisage difficulties," Arman assured her. "Judges are overworked and short delays are normal. Do some shopping, a bit of sightseeing. I'll make sure the court hears your case first thing on Friday morning." He rubbed a thumb and forefingers together.

Kat thanked him and rose to leave. "Incidentally," she asked, "did you hear from Ted on the trademark ownership outside Bazakistan?"

"Yes, I had an email ten minutes ago," Arman said. "One moment." He took an iPhone from his pocket and thumbed through emails. "Here it is. A long list of countries where class 33 trademark rights for Snow Mountain are registered." He winced. "Oh dear, it's bad news. The brand is owned by the Snow Mountain Company only in Bazakistan. Everywhere else, it belongs to EWB Ltd."

"What's class 33?" Kat asked. "And who's EWB? Is it part of the Snow Mountain Company?"

"Class 33 is the trademark category for alcohol," Arman said. He fingered his closely clipped beard. "I've no idea about EWB. It sounds like an English company. I'll ask Ted to find out."

Kat was discomfited. The brand's split ownership added complexity to her quest to regain her inheritance. She decided to follow his advice. Retail therapy would improve her mood.

Outside, light snow had begun to fall. There were no cabs. A battered black Mercedes ground to a halt next to her.

"Taxi?" the driver asked.

Kat didn't answer. She looked around anxiously, shivering in the snow. There were no other vehicles in sight.

"American?" the driver asked, hopefully. He was a slim Bazaki lad, about her age.

"English," Kat said. "Kireniat Mall?"

He nodded. "Five dollars."

She opened the passenger door and sat on the worn leather seat next to him. In her childhood, she'd heard of gypsy taxis, the informal transport that appeared whenever a driver had spare time and a desire to earn extra cash. Her family would never use one, of course; there was no need, when both her parents drove.

"I practise English, okay?" the lad announced in a marked local accent. "Why you in Kireniat?"

"For work," Kat said.

"You work in shop? At the Mall?"

He quizzed her for a while, taking a route that she thought circuitous, but no matter. It was a fixed price, and she'd brought plenty of dollars anyway. She recalled they were accepted everywhere. Looking at the snow, she told him she would buy furs.

"My uncle's shop in Kireniat Mall is best," the driver said, offering to collect her later and return her to her hotel.

Like much of Kireniat, the Mall was brand new and glitzy. Fountains tinkled, classical music played, spotlights displayed expensive goods to their best advantage. It was a world away from the untidy bazaars that Kat remembered. She found the furrier and marvelled at the soft sables, snow leopard and wolfskin on display. Although unsentimental about animals, she was also realistic. Such furs might be practical in Bazakistan, but in London they would attract attention of the least admiring kind. She chose a long white leather coat and matching hat, negotiated a discount for dollars, and made a beeline for a few more boutiques. Humming along to the piped Stravinsky, she returned to the waiting Mercedes with her purchases.

"The Intercontinental?" her new friend asked.

"Sure," Kat said. She mused dreamily about chilling out in the hotel spa, perhaps visiting a nightclub later. Fatigue slowed her reactions. When her driver wove in and out of backstreets, she didn't think to question his route. She didn't even think, in the split second when the car

60

stopped at a red light and two more young men jumped in through the rear doors, that she should leap out. The lights changed, the driver locked the doors, and her chance of salvation passed.

Chapter 13 **Ken**

Ken Khan was stocky where Nurbolat Khan was slim, but otherwise the two men could have been twins. Their resemblance had often been remarked upon in their National Service days, especially as both were the same height, shared a surname and sported a soldier's crewcut. Ken, it was true, had grown his hair and sprouted a beard and moustache since then, but they were still mistaken for brothers. They had a similar outlook on the world too, especially the sensitive issue of Bazakistan's politics and its President. After leaving the Army to study English at Kireniat University, they plotted sedition late into the night over a bottle of vodka. Ken was used to considering Nurbolat an obedient disciple, which was perhaps why he couldn't quite believe the news.

"You did what?" he demanded, eyeing the young woman sleeping in his elderly Mercedes.

"I've kidnapped her," Nurbolat confirmed. "She's a rich Westerner, here on business. Once we ransom her, we'll make a fortune."

Ulan, one of the other two boys who'd gone out with Nurbolat, butted in. "You know how it is, Ken. The boys take a lot of risks holding up banks and grocery stores, and it's not bringing in enough money. We need more to buy weapons and communications equipment."

"It's too risky," Ken replied. He didn't need the complications, political and practical, that a foreign hostage would bring. With regret, he decided they were already past the point of no return. The girl had seen too much; she could describe his comrades and their car. "I'm going to take her into the forest and shoot her," he added. "Let wild animals dispose of the evidence."

"You're missing out on easy money, then," Nurbolat said.

Ken was still sceptical. "How much do you honestly think we'll get?" he asked. Nothing about their hostage indicated wealth, apart from a diamond ring that could be fake and a collection of bags from pricy boutiques. She didn't look Western, either. Her features were Russian, full-lipped, high-cheekboned, sensuous like his lover's. Ken's thoughts drifted to Marina. He didn't want her to find out they'd kidnapped a pretty girl.

"Ten million dollars," Nurbolat said. "I tell you, she's rich. She's an English businesswoman and she's paying tens of thousands in bribes. She has told me this. There must be big money at stake. I have her passport too, and a thousand dollars in cash."

Ken whistled. They needed cash desperately. With money and time, they could spirit the woman over the border to another country before releasing her. They could buy guns. They could recruit mercenaries. "Fine," he said. "Let's do it."

Nurbolat flashed him a rare grin.

"And we must be organised," Ken said. He had to think quickly, address the practicalities. "Does she have a phone?"

"I've already switched it off," Nurbolat said.

"Good." His friend was bold, not rash. "Take it to the Kireniat Mall and switch it on again there in one of the coffee shops," Ken told him. "There are thousands of shoppers in that place every day, in a confined space. The militia won't find you, even if they're looking. Find out who her close family are and email a ransom demand from her phone."

Nurbolat nodded agreement.

"Make it plain they're not to tell the authorities," Ken said. "The British government stops ransoms being paid. We don't want them on the case, especially as our beloved President would have the militia look even harder for us."

"I understand that," Nurbolat said. "You can rely on me, Ken."

"We'll have to sort out logistics," Ken said. "My wife's in London, as you know. I'll get her to open a Swiss bank account. She can use it to buy arms as well. By the way, why is the girl asleep?"

Nurbolat and Ulan exchanged glances with their friend, Sultan. He'd stayed silent until now.

"Heroin," Sultan, said sheepishly.

If he'd had a gun in his pocket, Ken would have shot Sultan there and then. The girl would have died if they'd given her an overdose. "We smuggle that stuff. We don't use it," Ken said.

Sultan evaded his eyes.

"You injected her, I suppose," Ken stormed. "How come you had the equipment, and what possessed you, anyway? You could have killed her."

"She was like a fiend from hell," Ulan said sulkily. "She would have scratched Nurbolat's eyes out before we were even outside Kireniat. Then we'd all have died, because he was driving."

63

Ken's agitation lessened. What was the problem? The girl was alive. She'd have no idea where she was or how she'd got there, along a three mile dirt track through woods by the highway south of Kireniat. "All right. I understand. Actually, let's keep her drugged to confuse her senses." It would reduce the risk of identification and betrayal. "Use something less dangerous next time. Valium, Rohypnol, whatever. It can be slipped into her food and drink." He'd deal with Sultan's evident addiction later.

He noticed Ulan prick up his ears at the mention of Rohypnol. "No funny business," he warned. "We're freedom fighters, not rapists. I didn't want a hostage in the first place. It seems I have no choice, but the least I can do is treat her properly. Keep her quarters warm, give her food and sanitation, and keep your hands to yourselves." He glared at Ulan. "Remember, we can't kill the golden goose." Not yet, anyway. He wanted the gold first.

Chapter 14 **Marty**

Arystan Aliyev had once been a handsome young man. Marty remembered the slim, blond engineer he'd first met more than twenty years before. Harry had been Sasha Belov's second in command then. His looks were nearly gone, buried under the florid skin and bulbous nose of an alcoholic. The waxed hair was grey and thinning, the athletic figure run to fat. Harry's enthusiasm for engineering remained undimmed, however.

"We'll be expanding the production line here," he said, guiding Marty to a storage area at the back of the factory, a Soviet-era concrete box a few miles outside the city.

Marty nodded. After brief greetings in English, they'd switched to conversing in Russian. Marty was reasonably fluent. He had a gift for languages, and Harry's English was somewhat halting. "What about raw materials?" he asked. "Can you draw enough water from the stream?" Locally renowned for its pure water, the brook outside the distillery flowed straight from the foothills of the snow-capped peaks near Kireniat.

"Of course," Harry said. "And if not…" he showed Marty a new purification plant. "I designed it," he said proudly.

They went outside, ostensibly for Marty to view the vigour of the stream. Harry fumbled in his pocket for cigarettes, a local brand, and a lighter. Smoking was forbidden inside the factory. Marty suspected the rule was honoured only on occasions like this.

"Want a drink?" Harry asked, producing a quarter bottle of Snow Mountain vodka from another pocket.

"No, thanks," Marty said. "Not before five thirty."

Harry tipped half the bottle down his throat before lighting up. Marty half expected a magic trick, Harry breathing out a flame perhaps, but nothing extraordinary occurred. Harry simply stood silently, drawing on his cigarette, a superannuated James Dean.

"I'll give you a bottle for the road," Harry said. "Now tell me why you're here in Kireniat. I had no idea you were coming until you telephoned this morning."

Kireniat was small and close-knit enough that news travelled like wildfire. Marty decided it was pointless trying to keep a secret from his Bazaki business partner. "I'm looking for land to grow darria. Not in the mountains, but the valleys in between."

"Darria, huh?" Harry said. "The old wives' shrub. My wife drinks the tea every morning. She's tried to get me to do it, but hell will freeze over first. That stuff tastes foul."

"My wife likes it too," Marty admitted. "As soon as she heard it was full of anti-oxidants, she couldn't drink enough."

"Vanity triumphs over common sense," Harry remarked. "Anyway, you're buying land. What's your budget?"

"Two hundred thousand dollars."

Harry laughed. "When you first came here, that would have bought you the whole of Kireniat," he said. "It will still stretch a long way. There's a farm next to my summer house on sale for half that amount."

"Would that be Sasha's old summer house?" Marty asked. He recalled warm, sunny evenings, the smell of woodsmoke and roast meat, as he joined the family for barbecues. Sasha's wife, Maria, had been a fine cook and pretty with it; Kat was her spitting image.

"It would," Harry said, without appearing troubled in any way.

"I've a visit to that farm lined up tomorrow," Marty said.

Their eyes were drawn to the wood-clad bungalow next to the factory. Large, with picture windows, it had been built in the 1960s for the then factory manager. Sasha, and now Harry, lived there subsequently.

The building was surrounded by a garden of almost an acre, obviously well-tended despite the difficulties of the Kireniat micro-climate. Beyond the trees at the perimeter, only just in bud and still skeletal from winter, Marty saw a swish of blonde hair at the window.

Harry noticed it too. He waved. The blonde disappeared. "My wife," Harry explained. "She's shy."

Marty believed him. He'd never met Mrs Aliyeva. "How long have you been married now?" he asked.

"Nine years," Harry said. "I loved her for much longer, but until then, I couldn't give her this." His arm swept around from the house to the factory. "She likes the good things in life," he added.

Marty almost felt sorry for him, before recollecting how Harry had chased women, bedding and discarding them ruthlessly in the decade before his marriage. He knew of three illegitimate children; there were bound to be more. Harry had even followed Maria around like a dog trailing after a bitch on heat. She, at least, had nothing to do with him, Marty was sure.

He really ought to tell Harry about Kat's arrival in Bazakistan. That, after all, was why he'd made the effort to meet his business partner today. He wondered how to broach the subject, but it transpired he didn't have to.

"Do you see anything of Sasha's daughter in London?" Harry asked.

"Coincidentally, she was on the same plane to Kireniat," Marty told him.

"I'm not surprised." Harry lit another cigarette, and puffed on it furiously. "She's launched a court application to take the Snow Mountain Company away from me, factory and all."

"Could she succeed?" Marty said, alarmed.

"Over my dead body." Harry's blue eyes were cold as ice. "I've got the right people on my payroll."

They stood in silence until Harry's cigarette was finished. The wind had begun to rise. A few flakes of snow were falling. "Tea?" Harry asked.

Marty yawned. Despite his snooze on the plane, jet lag was overtaking him. "Please," he said.

Harry ushered him inside, past the stills and pipes, to the corridor of offices where the factory was managed. The walls, panelled in local pine, had been freshly painted white. They were adorned with framed Snow Mountain advertising posters.

A raven-haired Bazaki girl, looking scarcely old enough to have left school, sat typing in the antechamber to Harry's rather luxurious office. She stood to greet them, revealing long legs under a black leather mini-skirt.

Not for the first time, Marty was struck by the beauty of young Bazaki women. "Hello," he said.

"My new secretary," Harry said, by way of introduction. "She'll make the tea."

"New secretary?" Marty echoed, feeling the full gaze of the young woman's sultry eyes as she returned to her seat. She crossed her legs. The hem of the leather mini-skirt moved another inch up her slender thighs. "What happened to Nadia?"

"She moved on," Harry said. "This is Inna."

Inna batted feathery lashes, the same raven hue as her sleek mane. She leaned forward, leaving little to imagine about her buxom figure. "You're from London, Marty? I think we should take a business trip there, Harry, don't you?"

Harry looked contentedly at Inna's cleavage. "Oh, yes," he murmured.

"Visit me any time," Marty said, switching to English, "but if the bab's expecting Buckingham Palace, she'll be sadly disappointed. I'm based in Birmingham, which is, oh, a mere hundred miles away."

"I know," Harry said. "Do you think I can't tell the difference? I just plan to combine business with pleasure on my next visit to the UK. You understand me?"

"Too well," Marty winked. Harry hadn't changed.

Chapter 15 **Ken**

It was the safest of safe houses, because apart from Marina, only Ken's trusted inner circle knew of it.

Anyone who bothered to take the unpromising track through the forest would find a simple smallholding. It was just a little piece of land, an apple orchard with a few tumbledown buildings, but it was his. A son of the soil, Ken Khan loved the land with his bones. He'd spent too long away from it, displaced to the city after his parents' farm was expropriated. This was like coming home.

He was fond of Marina too. She'd brought him here; it was thanks to her that he had this place. The least he could do was light a fire for her, to make her comfortable. He gathered kindling from the woodpile and began igniting it in the grate; tentative flames at first, then a conflagration, sizzling and popping. This, he thought, was how democracy started. A few pinpoints of light in the darkness, gradually joining until the bright blaze consumed all obstacles in its path.

He heard the sound of an engine, wheels clattering along the dirt track. Eagerly, he ran to greet her.

Marina emerged from her Mercedes, a whirl of flashing eyes, blonde hair and white fur. Her boots crunched on the frozen ground. Her breath made clouds in the air. "It's been so long, Ken." She pulled him to her, kissing him passionately and stroking his waxed black hair. He'd allowed it to grow longer, so it fell back into the nape of his neck, the way she liked it.

"It's been only a week." He enveloped her in a bear hug. Her furs were soft and downy beneath his fingers. She smelled of lilies and love and mystery. She'd told him this was Chanel.

Anna, who cared for the pigs and chickens, wandered past, glaring pointedly. She disappeared into the hut where the English girl was manacled.

Ken had no intention of allowing Marina to follow, even in the unlikely event she wanted to. He took her hand, leading her inside to the heated room.

"This old shack's looking good," she said, removing her boots and shrugging off her coat.

Ken nodded. He and his friends had repaired the properties, whitewashing them inside and out. Within, this one was spotless and simply furnished: a single mattress, cushions on the floor. Colourful rugs covered both walls and floors. The scent and crackle of the fire filled the air.

Marina sat cross legged on the mattress. Ken snuggled into her, nuzzling the warm, clean skin of her neck. After a while, he undressed her, admiring her pale body, firm and white as a marble statue. How old was she? Anna had contemptuously told him that his mistress was in her fifties. He didn't believe it. He wasn't quite thirty himself. Marina was perhaps ten years his elder.

They'd met when he took a summer job in the distillery as a student. The affair survived his marriage to one of his classmates. Marina saw to that, such was her desperation for him. She needed him for the tenderness Aliyev wouldn't give her. For Ken too, since his wife fled to London, Marina was his only lover.

Unlike Marina and Aliyev, their forebears among the millions of Russians banished to Bazakistan by Stalin, Ken was of Bazaki origin. He was proud of his heritage: his swarthy skin, waxed hair and moustache, strapping figure. Marina liked them too. Her response was very unlike a statue as he made love to her, caressing her and making her moan with pleasure. He tried not to think of Aliyev doing the same.

Afterwards, he lit her cigarette before taking one for himself. As ever, she puffed gently while he took long, deep drags.

"Why don't you inhale?" he asked

"You only just noticed?" she said, amused. "My mother told me. Don't inhale, and you'll cheat the grave. And drink darria tea." She drew on her cigarette again. "Darria grows wild all around my dacha, actually. So much so, that an Englishman, Marty Bridges, wants to farm the shrub there. He's buying the land next to mine to do it."

"What does he want with darria?" Ken asked. It was akin to cultivating thistles and dandelions. Anyone could do it, but it was pointless.

"To sell the tea across the world," Marina said. "To steal our birthright, a natural Bazaki herb, to make himself rich. Worse still, he'll destroy the tranquillity of my bolthole. I'll be unable to snatch time with you there when Arystan's away on business in London." Her green eyes welled with tears. "You must get rid of Bridges, Ken. His death is the only solution."

"Murder him?" Once again, he pictured himself in the forest, dragging his victim to a quiet spot. A well-targetted bullet, carrion left for wolves to find; after they'd feasted, no one would know. Yet he was uneasy. The girl was different, because she'd been presented to him as a fait accompli. He would do what he needed to do, but why take unnecessary risks when, politically, he must keep his hands clean? On the day of the revolution, he needed foreign governments on side. "I can't do it," he told his lover.

He didn't understand why she hated the Englishman so much that she wanted him, of all people, dead. She'd never asked Ken to dispatch Aliyev, although she'd repeated frequently enough that she had no passion for the factory owner.

The tears fell faster now, droplets moistening her lashes. She pleaded. "Why can't you do this little thing for me? You've told me you'd slit the President's throat without a second thought."

"After a fair trial," Ken said. He had it planned: a showpiece trial to demonstrate the President's dreadful crimes to the international community, followed by a swift execution.

Marina persisted. "Please, Ken, do it for me. I'll give you anything you desire."

What did he need most? Guns, he supposed, but she couldn't supply those. "Your car," he said.

She laughed. "Have you written off the last one already?"

"Not quite," he said, unwilling to explain why the usefulness of the old black Mercedes was coming to an end. His men had taken it on bank raids too often, and now they'd kidnapped a foreigner in it. They'd been lucky, but it couldn't last. One day, the militia would notice that car and follow them. He was no Nelson Mandela. He didn't want to start a revolution from a prison cell.

"If that's what it takes, my car is yours," she said. "I'll tell Arystan I crashed it. He'll have to buy me another." She handed over the keys. "Here, you'll have to drive me into Kireniat."

Chapter 16 **Marty**

The young man from Kireniat's biggest real estate firm was insistent. "The appointment's in my diary," he said.

"And in mine," Marty retorted, "but not until this afternoon."

They were arguing in the lobby of his hotel, a Bazaki chain slightly less luxurious than the Intercontinental, and half the price. Marty had just emerged from the breakfast room, glad Angela wasn't with him. She would undoubtedly have chided him for eating too much. After several raids on the buffet and copious cups of coffee, Marty was over his jet lag. He relented. "All right," he said. "I don't have anything else planned for the morning. I'll get my coat."

It was a Barbour quilted parka, which Marty considered a superior British alternative to the furs and sheepskins favoured by rich Bazakis. He was always telling Harry this. Marty decided it was prudent to wear boots as well. At this time of year, a sunny morning in Kireniat could suddenly give way to snow.

The lad introduced himself as Roman Popov, a surprisingly Russian-sounding name for an ethnic Bazaki, and led the way to his car.

Marty was impressed. The silver Mercedes glinted in the sunshine, not a dent in sight. Its cream leather seats were pristine. "You've done well for yourself, haven't you?" he said.

"I am Salesman of the Year," Roman said, smirking beneath his waxed moustache and beard. "In fact, I'm supposed to be training a couple of young associates today. Would you mind if I drop by the office to collect them?"

"No problem," Marty said. "Do they speak English as well as you do?"

"Of course," Roman replied.

Marty doubted it. He knew the Bazakis were likely to speak privately in another tongue. Their conversation might reveal enough to secure a better deal, perhaps even access to a wider range of properties. For now, as usual when making new business contacts abroad, he kept his linguistic skills to himself.

Roman had a short conversation on his phone. "We'll pick them up at the railway station," he said.

Marty settled into the passenger seat next to Roman, declining the proffered cigarettes. While he preferred his Jag, this car was perfectly

comfortable for a forty minute journey. Roman lit up and drove to the
web of backstreets next to the main railway station. He stopped by a
phone shop. Two men, young and suited like him, opened the Merc's rear
doors.

"Hop in," Roman said. "Marty, my colleagues, Alex and Vlad."

There were handshakes and how-do-you-dos before the car sped
away, slipping swiftly onto the highway out of the city.

"The knife, Nurbolat." Vlad's words were delivered in Bazaki.

Marty unconsciously flung his head forward. "What's going on?" he
shouted.

Roman seemed puzzled. "Is there a problem, Marty?" he asked.

Despite the constraint of his seatbelt, Marty twisted round in time to
see Alex lunging towards him. A blade glittered in the young man's hand.
Without sparing a second to think, Marty landed a punch on Alex's nose.
It broke with an audible crack. Alex dropped his knife.

Marty reached for the door handle, just as one of the men – he wasn't
sure who – retrieved the knife and held it to his neck.

"Keep still," Roman warned him, "Or we'll slit your throat."

Alex sniffed and moaned.

"What do you want from me?" Marty asked.

"Only your co-operation," Roman said. "We will blindfold you, and if
you're sensible, you won't resist. We don't mean you any harm."

"You could have fooled me," Marty said bitterly. "Get that joker to
put his weapon away."

Roman issued a few words of instruction. The pressure of cold metal
vanished from Marty's neck. A cloth was bound around his head.
Darkness filled his eyes.

Marty wondered what was happening. He hadn't offended the local
mafia, as far as he knew, and Harry was far too smart an operator to have
done so. If this was a mugging, it was elaborate and slow – unless they
were simply driving off the beaten track, to rob and kill him away from
prying eyes. The good suits, and luxury car, meant nothing; they could be
stolen.

Roman appeared to confirm it. "You've made a bad enemy, Marty.
What have you done that someone wants you dead?"

"I've no idea," Marty said. "Don't play games. You told me you
didn't intend any harm." He maintained a calm voice, despite his
mounting terror.

Roman didn't react. "It surely can't be just because you're buying some farmland, can it?" he asked.

"You tell me," Marty said, baffled. Although he'd annoyed a few club owners on his home turf in Birmingham, none would go this far, in any sense. Within Bazakistan, he had no enemies. He hadn't crossed Harry, his only contact in the local business community. Anyway, Harry needed him. It was thanks to Marty that Snow Mountain was successful, and Marty was a convenient excuse for Harry's trips abroad.

Kat was here in Kireniat, though, with money enough to pay for a contract killing. Marty felt nauseous. He heard ringing in his ears. Right now, his blood pressure was heading skywards, and he wouldn't be surprised if a heart attack snuffed out his life before they put a bullet in his head. Was that what Roman had in mind? Or would Alex use his knife? There were an infinite number of nasty, brutal ways to kill a man. Which would they choose? He clawed at his blindfold.

"Stop that," Roman commanded. "Do as I say and I won't kill you. I was told to do it, but the price is too low. You're worth more to me alive." His tone became businesslike, akin to his earlier façade as a real estate agent. "At least, if your family loves you. You'd better hope they do, Marty, because they'll have to pay twenty million dollars for your release."

Marty felt his pulse rate drop a little at this reprieve. "That's too much. A million, tops," he said. The going rate for murder would be a fraction of that. He might as well negotiate the ransom down to maximise the chance of someone paying it. The product that Charles had sold him included kidnap insurance; he couldn't recall if there was a cap.

Roman laughed. "Don't try haggling. I'm not selling you a carpet."

"Why not?" Marty asked, fury beginning to bubble over his fear. "Why shouldn't you have a proper job, selling land or carpets or Bazaki handicrafts? I hadn't realised bandits were operating in the middle of Kireniat."

A vicious slap was delivered to his head. Marty reeled, seeing stars. He tried to remove the blindfold again. This time, rough hands grabbed his arms and pinioned them to the seat.

"Enough, Nurbolat," Roman said. "Let him speak. We're not bandits, Marty." His voice reflected injured pride. "We're freedom fighters."

"What kind of freedom would that be?" Marty asked. "The freedom to kidnap innocent people from the street and get rich by holding them hostage? Sounds like banditry to me."

There was no reply. Marty wondered if he'd gone too far, and with a sinking heart, wished he could retract his words. Roman had the others under control but he was dangerous in his own right; only a fool would push his patience to breaking point. He was about to apologise when Roman sighed.

"You don't understand, Marty," his captor replied. "The end justifies the means. We need money for munitions, mercenaries and bribes. We're going to bring down this corrupt government: the President and his land-grabbing cronies. The dictator may think he can suppress dissent, and it's true he's slaughtered all the old guard who opposed him, but he'll never win. Young people like us are ready to overthrow him."

It was a fine speech, delivered with the passion of youth. Marty received it with the scepticism of middle age. "And then what?" he asked. "You'll simply replace one dictatorship with another. And when Bazakistan is part of your religious caliphate, all that precious foreign investment will vanish in the blink of an eye. Even if you allowed Harry Aliyev to carry on making vodka, which I doubt, I wouldn't bother coming here to buy it from him." He wouldn't grow darria here, either, as long as he could persuade the shrub to flourish anywhere else. Erik was right; Bazakistan wasn't stable enough.

"I'm not creating a totalitarian state," Roman protested, noticeably outraged. "I'm a Muslim, of course, but…"

One of the other lads tittered.

"All right," Roman snapped, "I don't pray or attend the mosque, but nor do any of you. Be quiet." He regained his composure. "Do you think, Marty, that Da'esh haven't made overtures to me? They'd gladly give me all the money, weapons and men I could ever want. And in return, they'd require that I deliver Bazakistan back to the Stone Age. Butcher my Russian friends, deny an education to my nieces, repress all the idiots who decided to stay rather than flee over the border. I would never do that. Never," he repeated. "And that, my friend, is why I need you. You're a valuable commodity. I won't hurt you – as long as you behave."

The radio blared into life with a loud, cheesy pop melody. One of the men whistled along tunelessly. They certainly didn't behave like religious fanatics, but that didn't lessen his jeopardy. Marty took the music as a cue that Roman no longer wished to speak. Indeed, once the whistling ceased, the men were silent for the remainder of the journey. Eventually, the car left the highway, bumping and clattering along what was obviously a rough track. It came to an abrupt halt. As the doors were opened, a blast of icy air assailed him.

"We're going to tie your hands and feet," Roman said. "Not too much, and not too tight. You will understand."

Marty was dragged out of the Mercedes. Outside the car, it was chilly. The ground was hard underfoot; possibly frozen grass rather than tarmac. His arms were thrust in front of him and tied together roughly at the wrists. Rope shackles were placed around his ankles, enabling him to shuffle, but no more. He felt his pockets being emptied.

"This is the right man," he heard Roman say, seconds after his passport and wallet were removed.

Stumbling, Marty was manhandled to a building and shoved inside. His wrists were untied; then knotted again, this time leaving two feet of rope between them. He heard a door close, a key turn in a lock.

"You may remove your blindfold," Roman instructed, his voice muffled by the heavy wooden door between them.

Marty swung his bound arms upwards towards his face. His hands tore at the cloth covering his eyes, pulling it away. He blinked, dazzled by the sudden light.

He was standing near the door and window of an oblong room perhaps twelve by twenty feet, and just high enough to stand. His captors had tied his feet to the doorpost. At the opposite end of the room, out of reach, a fire blazed in a black tin stove. There was no furniture other than rugs and hangings on the wall and floors, a few blankets and a bucket.

Someone behind him tapped his arm. He spun round, prepared to fight for his life.

"Hello, Marty," Kat said.

Her hands and feet were bound like his. Although she might want his blood, she was in no position to engage an assassin. If she hadn't done it, then who had?

76

Chapter 17 **Kat**

It was a really strange dream, and unpleasant. There was a Mongol horde, riding across the plains on horses that turned into Mercedes cars. There was a whitewashed farmhouse, a sad girl surrounded by pigs. Lastly, there was Marty Bridges, the businessman who could have saved her father's skin, but chose to build his bank balance instead.

"Hello, Marty," she said, hoping she would wake up in her hotel bedroom, and Marty would dissolve into dust like all nightmares.

He didn't. "Kat, are you all right?" he said.

No, she wasn't. She was exhausted, curiously unrefreshed despite the sleeping and dreaming. She shrank back into the corner, onto her knees. If only she could just close her eyes again.

Marty wouldn't let her. It wasn't fair. He was holding the lids open, even though his fingers and hands were restricted in their movement because his wrists were tied together with rough jute rope.

She gasped. Marty's eyes were unexpectedly compassionate. A piercing blue, they blazed with concern for her.

"Your pupils are pinpoints," he said, his voice somehow distant. "Something's very wrong. Kat, what have they done to you?"

She tried to say she'd been running away, across the plains and through the orchard outside. She wanted to run from the laughing men, the sad girl and the farmhouse. The words stuck in her throat. It filled with bile. She placed her bound hands in front of her mouth.

"You need the bucket." The new, shiny, wise, kind Marty, a phantom in her dream, brought it in front of her. He helped her kneel over it, tenderly holding her hair back as she vomited.

Chapter 18 **Marty**

The room stank of puke. Satisfied Kat had finished, Marty moved the bucket as far away from him as he could. She was shivering, although she wore a dark business suit and the stove was warm. He picked up a blanket. It was dark red and coarse; probably horsehair. He tucked it around her.

Outside, he could hear voices: men, and occasionally, a woman. Their words were indistinct. From a small high window, he could see more squat, whitewashed buildings. Birdsong and other animal noises suggested a farm. He tried to estimate how long he'd spent in the car. They could be no more than forty miles outside Kireniat, but in which direction, it was impossible to guess.

Gradually, Kat began to thaw, her eyes regaining focus. "Marty," she said, "what are you doing here?"

It was a good question. Did he buy Roman's story about a kidnap for ransom? He was alive, which suggested there was some truth in it.

His reply to Kat was wry. "Welcome to the Hotel California, bab. Ensuite bucket, Bazaki lads on hand to ignore your every whim, and no mod cons. I'm not saying you can never leave, but it'll cost you a pretty penny." He waved his bound wrists in front of her. "My wife will be getting a ransom demand soon, and I bet Mr Millionaire Ross Pritchard has had one already."

"How much?" she asked.

Marty whistled. "Ten, twenty million dollars. I hope Ross bought kidnap insurance for you. His company sold me plenty."

Kat's pale face looked strained. She drew the blanket tighter around her shoulders.

"He didn't, then?" Marty said. "That was careless of him, wasn't it? Being an insurance expert and all."

"What will happen if he doesn't pay?"

Marty couldn't believe she was serious. "He's a rich man, Kat. That's why you're marrying him, isn't it?" He didn't wait for her to protest, although he noticed she opened her mouth. He added, "Of course Ross will pay. He loves you. He bought you that huge chunk of rock."

Her eyes grew tender as she examined the sparkling ring on her right hand. "They haven't taken it," she said.

Marty considered her words. "These lummocks claim they're revolutionaries rather than thieves," he said. "They want to bring down the government."

"It's about time," Kat said, unexpectedly.

There was a knock on the door.

"How polite our new friends are," Marty observed. He lowered his voice to a whisper. "Kat, take my advice. Don't speak Russian to them. Or Bazaki. Unless they already know you can, keep that information to yourself."

"They don't know," she replied, nodding.

A Bazaki woman entered, glancing at them nervously before looking away. She was perhaps Kat's age, dressed in an anorak and jeans, her long black hair wild from the wind that blew into the shack with her. There was no trace of make-up, or of joy, on her striking face. She carried a tray set with two tin bowls of cabbage soup, spoons, flatbreads, two mugs of milkless tea and a couple of scabbed red apples.

Marty pointed to the bucket, its stench almost causing his own stomach to heave. "Can you take this away please, young lady?" he demanded.

While she remained silent, she certainly understood his meaning. Laying her tray on the floor a few feet away from them, she picked up the bucket and took it with her. The door slammed behind her. Marty heard the key turn once, then again a few minutes later. She reappeared with the same bucket, shiny and damp from being washed, before leaving and locking them in again.

Marty gazed at Kat, gauging if she had an appetite. He had none. It was not so long since his large breakfast. He took an apple and put it in his pocket for later, just in case.

"Kat, can you eat?" he asked kindly. "Keep your strength up, bab."

"I'll sip tea," she said, a wan grin forming. "There's no better place to drink tea than Bazakistan. They really know how to brew a cup."

Marty recalled Erik and the sweet, dark tea they drank together. If he had a preference, it was for the English builders' version. "You go ahead," he said.

Kat drained a tin mug quickly. She took a tentative spoonful of soup, then another, before announcing it was delicious, and finishing the bowl.

Marty had reservations about her claim. Cabbage soup was the kind of meal Angela would serve on a fast day, virtually ensuring Marty wouldn't ingest any calories. "Have the other bowl too," he offered. "I'm not hungry."

Kat fell to it, eating half the bread as well. Colour returned to her cheeks. "How are we going to get out of here?" she asked. "Have you got your phone?"

Marty shook his head. "Everything was taken."

He checked his pockets, and she did the same, finding them empty as predicted.

"What about the ropes?" she asked. "Can you untie me?"

Marty grinned. "I can try."

He picked at the knots around her hands. His short fingernails made virtually no impact, but a spoon handle gave him more leverage. Unfortunately, the Bazaki girl caught him in the act when she returned for the tray. Swearing in her local tongue, she summoned Roman and Alex. The latter, a bandage over his nose, scowled at Marty.

Marty was more concerned about the Kalashnikov that Roman was pointing at him. He listened intently to the heated discussion among their captors. Although they spoke in Bazaki, the foreign language and Kireniat dialect posed no problem for him.

"I told you they were more trouble than they were worth," the girl spat.

"You cannot be serious," Alex replied. "They're a goldmine."

"If they're as rich as you say," she said.

"I have it on the best authority," Roman said. "If I'm wrong, I'll take full responsibility for the consequences."

"We should be chaining them up," Alex said. "I've brought everything we need, as you well know."

"Very well," Roman agreed. "We can't take risks. I'd hoped for more co-operation from our guests, but it seems I won't get it." He switched to English, addressing Marty and Kat. "I repeat. Behave, and you won't get hurt. Just to make sure, I'm putting you in chains."

Roman and his gun remained in position as Alex made trips to fetch chains, padlocks and a drill. Roman's henchman fixed a heavy metal ring next to the window, then replaced the ropes with chains and padlocks. Alex used a figure of eight on each of hands and feet, allowing limited room to manoeuvre. A longer chain bound them to a short radius from the window, like dogs on a leash.

Kat submitted to her shackles with a sullen expression. Marty didn't resist either. Tempted as he was to joke about the famous Bazaki hospitality, he decided this wasn't the right time to antagonise his captors. He couldn't escape anyway. The window was far too small and the door bound to be locked.

Satisfied their captives were secured, the kidnappers left, with a final threatening glare from Alex.

"At least we've got a clean bucket," Marty said.

Kat was subdued. "I feel so tired," she yawned. She lay on the pile of blankets, cocooning herself in one of them.

Marty watched her doze. He felt her forehead. There was no sign of a temperature, but something was amiss. Their gaolers must have drugged the food, perhaps the tea as well. Kat had eaten his portion of soup too, he realised. He resolved to leave his next meal untouched and urge Kat to do the same, however appetising it appeared.

No one could easily tinker with an apple, though. He felt it in his pocket and was comforted, knowing he could turn to it when hunger and thirst overwhelmed him.

Marty used the bucket, briefly grateful that Kat was asleep. Smoke from the smouldering stove overcame the smell, but the room was becoming stifling. He opened the tiny window a fraction. A welcome breeze, fragrant with honey blossom, wafted inside. The cold snap that had greeted him in Kireniat had vanished.

He heard a car approach, and halt. A door slammed, locking with a beep. Stilettos clacked across the yard.

"Kat!" he shouted, shocked. For a moment, he stared, puzzled that she'd suddenly appeared outside. The illusion was swiftly dispelled. He looked down and saw at once that he was wrong; his fellow hostage lay at his feet still, asleep and oblivious.

The woman outside glanced round at his cry. Seeing nothing, she flicked her long blonde hair around her fur-clad shoulders, and slipped through the door of the farmhouse opposite.

Marty felt his hands tremble beneath their makeshift cuffs. The visitor could have been Kat's twin, or an older sister. That was impossible, he knew. He'd socialised with Sasha and Maria often enough, acting like an uncle to their two children during their education in England. If the family had been larger, he would have known. This was no sister. It could only be Sasha's widow, Maria.

He'd believed her dead, but how could he really tell? She'd simply stopped communicating with him, after he'd sent her almost a hundred thousand pounds for legal fees and bribes to secure Sasha's release from gaol. That was all to no avail, of course. Sasha's death had been announced after two years in the hell-hole to which the implacable Bazaki courts had consigned him.

On the other hand, Maria's death wasn't made public, nor had Marty seen a death certificate. Harry had delivered the news during their early communications, when both wanted Marty to maintain his Snow Mountain vodka distribution business, despite their lack of trust in each other.

Marty dug his nails into the palms of his hands. This was too bizarre. More likely, despite Angela's attempt to train him with her diet, his self-imposed fast was causing him to hallucinate. His eyes rested on Kat again. He must have imagined the other woman shared her features. There were thousands of Russian blondes here; millions even. Finally, desperate to banish the image from his mind, he took the apple from his pocket and ate every last scrap, pips and all.

Sounds in the yard outside were clearer now the window was open. Marty heard footsteps and peeked through the glass. The girl who'd brought the food was smoking with Alex.

"Marina Aliyeva is here again," she said. There was no mistaking the contempt in her voice.

Marty jumped backwards, almost tripping over.

Alex laughed. "Leave it, Anna. There's no chance for you with Ken, you know that. He's in love."

Her own laughter was hollow. "Love? He's her pampered lapdog. Anything he wants, she gives him. This orchard, a car – two cars now..."

Alex interrupted her. "We needed a hideout, and transport," he said. "Ken and I are on the run, remember? He does what he has to do. It all helps the cause." He licked his lips. "It wouldn't bother me, either, if she liked me. She's a fine-looking woman."

"She's old, Nurbolat." Anna was dismissive.

Marty noted the name she used. Their leader wasn't called Roman either, he reckoned. His money would be on Ken. Was this the revolutionary Erik had mentioned?

Anna took a drag on her cigarette before confirming it. "What makes you think I'm interested in Ken Khan? He's married," she said.

"You complain too much," Nurbolat said. His chuckle was ribald. "Ken's wife is in exile. Why shouldn't he let an old dog teach him new tricks? If he needs help handling her, I'd volunteer."

"Be careful what you wish for," Anna said darkly. "Aliyev's wife has seen off one husband already. She's too much of a woman for you."

"You can never have too much of a woman," Nurbolat said, cupping his upturned palms in front of him. "Marina Aliyeva has breasts to die for."

"Perhaps you'll find out," Anna said nastily.

Nurbolat told her to stick to feeding the pigs. Glowering, she stamped out her cigarette and stormed out of view.

It was hours before Marina emerged from the farmhouse, a flushed glow upon her face. Marty scrutinised her features carefully, comparing them with Kat's. The smile, slightly long nose and oval face were the same. He was too far away to see the colour of Marina's eyes.

Kat was beginning to stir. "What are you looking at?" she asked. She was still groggy.

"Nothing." Although suspicion raged within him, he didn't want to share it with her. How could he give her hope that her mother was alive, when he didn't really know? Suppose he was wrong?

The food was another matter. "They're drugging us," he told Kat. "There were sleeping pills in the soup or the tea. Maybe both."

"So we can't eat?" she said.

"See what they bring us," he told her.

As dusk fell, Anna brought meat stew and more flatbread, apples and tea. Marty's mouth watered at the savoury aroma. He was thirsty, too. Nevertheless, he poured all the tea into the bucket.

"Keep the mugs. We'll stick them out of the window when it rains," he said.

They agreed the flatbread and apples were safe to eat. The food hardly touched the sides. Hungrily, they watched as Anna removed the plates of stew. The girl shook her head at them.

The window darkened, leaving the stove's embers their only source of illumination. The room had no electric light; it was little more than a shed.

"Good night, Marty," Kat said.

He helped her choose a blanket before taking one for himself. The rest, he heaped into mounds to give her the semblance of a mattress and pillow. She soon fell asleep, although as he lay there wakefully, he heard her rise. While she tiptoed to the bucket, her chains clanked. He pretended to be dozing.

Wolves howled in the distance. Marty lay on a rug, his mind churning late into the night, the chains chafing him. Even when he slept, Harry, Marina and Ken stalked his dreams.

Chapter 19 **Davey**

"Are you still here?" Davey said. "It's time you were going home."

It was only 2pm, but Ross shouldn't have been in the office at all. Pallid, sweating and pumped full of painkillers, he was clearly unwell. He'd arrived at eleven to help Davey add the finishing touches to a pitch he was making to a large multinational.

"How did it go?" Ross asked. His desk, usually tidy to the point of OCD, was littered with empty coffee cups and packets of pills.

"We got the sale," Davey said, smiling. "They liked the pitch, they liked the view from the Duck & Waffle, and most of all they liked the wine. We all had rather too much of it." Although his new client's headquarters were in Luxembourg, he'd conducted business over lunch at the upscale restaurant at the top of the Heron Tower. He often invited prospective clients there. The food was exquisite, there were impressive views over the City of London, and it wasn't far for him to stagger back to his office on the seventeenth floor.

Ross was clearly relieved. "Great. I'll just pack up then, and get a cab back. Oh – excuse me." His phone was ringing.

Charles gave Davey a high five. All three men shared an office, an airy space with pleasant enough views of its own. They hardly noticed the vista over London any more, though. It had become like wallpaper to them.

"What do you mean?" Ross said to the caller. "It's a joke, right?" His face, already pale from his illness, was white.

"I suppose Kat's pregnant," Charles hissed, as Ross continued his tense conversation, oblivious to their speculation.

"That's my guess, too," Davey admitted. He grinned. "Two new fathers in the office? The girls will say it's something in the water." He hadn't spoken to Charles about Dee's baby yet. The lunchtime claret was loosening his tongue.

Charles' eyes softened, then he winced. "I've barely seen George."

Davey didn't reply. It wasn't appropriate to become involved in Charles and Dee's relationship, or lack of one, however much he sympathised with his IT director.

"It was a gory birth," Charles added, shuddering at the memory. "I was gasping for a smoke afterwards."

"I heard," Davey said. "I presume Dee was ice-cool. Planning a series of baby yoga videos, perhaps. She seems to regard pregnancy as a business opportunity." He chuckled. "I could almost imagine her booking the studio and cameras, then choosing you to father the child."

Charles' cheeks flamed. "I've considered that," he said stiffly. "As a matter of fact, I raised it with Dee. She's been rather cold towards me, actually."

"Yes," Davey said, thinking Charles could have used more tact.

"I appreciate I didn't improve matters by saying it," Charles pointed out. "How is she, anyway?"

"In great shape," Davey said. "You wouldn't know she'd just given birth." Laura had never slimmed down to her wedding weight once their offspring had arrived. "You know Dee. Breastfeeding, vitamin pills, yoga – she says the pounds peel off." He thought Charles looked uncomfortable. "Why don't we break out the bourbon? Hey, we can all use a drink. We should celebrate the new contract."

He'd acquired a taste for the whiskey since his first night with Alana. As he poured a slug into Charles' coffee mug, he thought longingly of incendiary sex with her. Maybe he could see her that evening, tell Laura that he had to stay in London to work late again.

"Ross looks like he could use some of that, too," Charles said.

Davey was about to find a glass for the actuary, when he glimpsed the boxes of pills on Ross' desk once more. "I don't think so," he said, motioning to them. "Let's keep him in one piece."

Ross finished the call, and immediately speed-dialled another number. "Call me straight away, darling," he said, placing the phone on his desk, and putting his head in his hands.

"What's up?" Davey asked.

"Kat's been kidnapped," Ross said. "They want ten million dollars."

"How?" Davey stared, shocked, at Ross' grim face. "Where is she?"

"Bazakistan," Ross said bitterly. "It's where she comes from."

"Why on earth would she go there?" Davey asked, puzzled. He was aware that Kat had been orphaned as a child, and the Bazaki government was somehow responsible. It seemed the last place she would visit.

"She had a crazy notion of recovering the family business," Ross said. "She had to lodge a claim in person at a court in Kireniat. Her brother was urging her not to go. I tried to talk her out of it too, but she wouldn't listen. In the end, I gave in."

Davey imagined Kat could be persuasive. "Look, you must tell the police," he said. "Get the Foreign Office involved."

"They'll kill her if I tell the authorities," Ross said. Already ill, he appeared to be on the point of collapse.

"Are you sure this is for real?" Charles asked gently. "It could be a version of one of those holiday scams. I know she didn't answer her phone, but it could have been stolen, couldn't it?"

"She may be a free woman, walking through the streets of Bazaku City as we speak," Davey said.

"No," Ross said. "The phone call was from my lawyer friend, Ted Edwards. His correspondent law firm in Kireniat received the ransom demand, with a photo. He's going to email it."

"Well, let's see it," Davey said. "Have you received it yet?"

"Not here." Ross looked up at his laptop screen. "It will have gone to my personal email." He tapped his smartphone. "Here it is. Oh, God."

The picture showed a blonde woman, fully clothed but unconscious on a rug or large cushion, her hands and feet roped together.

Davey peered uncertainly at the tiny screen. "Hold on," he said. "Is that really her?"

"Let's see it on a bigger screen," Ross said, switching on his iPad.

The likeness was unmistakable. "If this is a fraud, someone's done something very clever with Photoshop," Charles concluded gloomily.

"If only I'd gone with her," Ross said. "I would have done, but for this wretched flu. She went alone. Now she's going to die unless I raise a sum of money that is, quite frankly, beyond my means."

"Could you sell your flat, or borrow against it?" Charles asked.

"It's not worth anything like that," Ross said. "Even if I sell my investments, I won't have enough. And they want it by next week. It's impossible. I can't find the money that quickly, not even by playing poker."

"Don't do that," Davey cautioned sharply. Ross was a legend in the industry for using his undoubted mathematical skills to win large sums playing poker, both online and in casinos. Even so, distraught and delirious with flu, he'd make mistakes and lose everything.

Despite his well-oiled lunch and afternoon bourbon, a sense of doom almost returned Davey to sobriety. An hour ago, he might have been envious of Ross: a gilded youth with money, a glittering career ahead, good looks and a gorgeous fiancée. Now, nothing would persuade him to swap places. Worse, he was powerless to help.

Chapter 20 **Marty**

A succession of short, sharp explosions of sound woke Marty from his uneasy dreams. Panicked, he curled into a ball, protecting his head as best his chains allowed.

White light flashed across the room, and heavy rain lashed at the window. Opening his eyes, he saw he and Kat were still alone. Once he realised he'd heard thunder rather than gunfire, his relief was sweet.

First light broke as he listened to the storm, his heart still pounding. Kat slumbered on, her features angelic. He forced himself to put comparisons with Marina Aliyeva out of his mind.

His stomach rumbled. He held both mugs out of the window, soon filling them, and drank from one. Predictably, it slaked his thirst, but no more.

A particularly loud retort of thunder roused Kat. She immediately screamed.

"It's only the weather," Marty said.

She peered at him, bleary-eyed. "I'm sorry," she said. "I dreamed I was in my hotel, ordering from room service, so I wasn't expecting to see you – or this." She gestured around the mean cell. "I'm so hungry," she complained.

"Sorry, bab," Marty said. "H_2O is all I can offer you." He gave her the other mug. "You'll have to pretend it's champagne, a special calorie-free version. That's important to you girls, isn't it?"

Kat snatched it, giving him a dirty look.

Refilling the mugs, he said, "They don't want to starve us. We're valuable merchandise, remember? Your legs are worth five million each."

"They're not insured, though, are they? Unlike yours," she said. "What if Ross can't pay?"

"He'll negotiate," Marty said. Whatever he thought of Ross, the lad wasn't stupid.

"They might kill us anyway," Kat said. Her lip twitched.

"No, if they wanted to, they'd have done it already," Marty said. She had a point, but he couldn't afford to concede it to her. If she was already on the edge of hysteria, it might tip her over the line. He didn't need that.

He was worried about Angela. He pictured her sitting alone in her spacious kitchen. She must have received a ransom demand by now, and would surely be out of her mind with anguish. Would she remember the insurance? Better to pay than rely on the Bazaki police to find him. Ken Khan had hidden his hostages too well.

A greater concern was Harry Aliyev. Marty's business partner knew better than anyone how to galvanise the Bazaki authorities into action. Had Angela told him Marty was missing? With his network, there was a chance he'd find out what was happening. That would be bad news for Marina Aliyeva. Yet it could be worse for Marty, because Harry would want rid of Kat, and he might think Marty's death was a price worth paying for that.

Kat turned away from him, and Marty decided it was actually for the best. They'd simply inflame each other's fears if he began another conversation.

He simmered restlessly until sunshine had finally dispelled the rainclouds and Anna arrived with food. It was a meal that Marty considered brunch, although it bore little relation to the hearty buffet at his hotel. Once again, she'd brought apples, bread and tea, this time with a grainy grey porridge.

"Is it drugged?" he demanded, eyeing the tray doubtfully.

Anna averted her gaze without replying. She probably didn't understand.

Marty was unwilling to break his cover by speaking Russian or Bazaki. "I bet it is," he continued. "Where's Ken Khan? I want to talk to him." He was raising his voice now, his patience exhausted. "Bring him here right now," he yelled, shaking his fist, even more frustrated by the impotence imposed by his shackles.

Kat stared at him, her expression guarded, as Anna stomped out of the door.

"Don't you start," he said to her.

Kat shrugged. "I didn't say anything." She looked at the tray. "Half that bread has your name on it. And an apple."

Marty realised how hungry he was and grabbed the tray, letting Kat help herself before devouring the chewy flatbread. His apple followed it. Regretfully, he pushed the porridge away. Angela's diet hadn't prepared him for two consecutive days of iron rations.

He heard Anna outside, shouting, "Ulan!" Eventually, she reappeared with the stocky young Bazaki who'd been introduced to Marty as Vlad.

"You tell them, Ulan," she said in her local tongue.

90

Ulan, ogling Kat impudently, had heavily accented and stilted English. "Ken is not here," he said.

"When will he be back?" Marty asked.

Ulan sniggered. "I know not," he said. With a final lustful gaze, he left. Anna picked up the tray and followed him.

"Didn't you want to slap him?" Marty asked Kat.

"What do you mean?" She looked puzzled.

"The way he gawped at you," Marty said. Sensing her total lack of comprehension, he said, "Never mind." Men probably eyed Kat like that all the time.

Kat lapsed into sullen silence. Marty, unrefreshed by the poor meal and fretful night, tried and failed to catch up on his sleep. He resorted to staring out of the window in an unsuccessful effort to stave off boredom, hunger and dread. Eventually, he decided bread, apples and rainwater weren't enough. However fantastical an escape might seem, it gave the hostages their best chance of survival. If they didn't gain sustenance, he and Kat would never have the physical or mental strength to find a way out.

"We should eat everything tonight," he said. "Who cares if there are sedatives in the stew? We need to sleep anyway."

She muttered acquiescence. When supper was brought, they both fell like wolves on the meaty stew, wiping their dishes clean with delicious flatbread. The accompanying tea tasted like nectar, better than any Marty had had in his life.

Prayers didn't come naturally to a man who acknowledged God only on high days or holidays. Still, as Marty drifted to sleep, he pleaded with his deity to spare his life. Whatever else he'd desired before, he'd settle for that now.

Chapter 21 **Davey**

The tension and misery of an angry heavy metal track matched Davey's sombre mood. Slowly, his stress eased and he forgot Ross' impossible dilemma. He was no longer a bald City gent braving the morning exhaust fumes of Bishopsgate, but transported back to his youth, wild curly locks bouncing around his face as he joined fellow headbangers at Wembley Stadium.

Another commuter jostled him. The spell was broken. Rush hour began early in the City. By 8am, the pavements were a mass of drab-suited City workers, all striding purposefully towards their offices. Davey spotted Charles easily. The IT director was the only man dawdling in the throng outside the Heron Tower. As Davey waved to him, Charles cast a cigarette stub away and lit another.

Davey raised an eyebrow. "I've never seen you do stress before, Charles."

Charles laughed bitterly. "Just wait until your children grow up." He took a long drag.

"I'll keep you company," Davey said, relieved that Charles' woes were apparently nothing to do with Dee. "What's up?"

Charles seemed hesitant, inhaling another lungful of smoke and glancing around anxiously before he replied. "You'll recall I sold some corporate risks insurance recently?" he whispered.

"Oh yes, when we were in Birmingham," Davey said. He, too, kept his voice low. There was no need to share information with passers-by. He dimly recollected the sale, although his memories of the conference were dominated by the whirlwind affair with Alana. Charles had crowed about his triumph at the time. "Your daughter works for the policyholder, doesn't she?"

"Indeed," Charles agreed. "She phoned me first thing this morning in a panic. I didn't even have a chance to tell her about George. She wanted to talk about a potential claim. It's serious."

Davey shrugged. Charles lived on his nerves too much. He supposed Amy was the same. "That's why we're in business. I don't see the problem."

"I may not have completed the paperwork correctly," Charles admitted.

Davey suspected he knew what was wrong. "Have you completed it at all?" he asked.

Charles' silence spoke volumes. Davey clapped a hand on his shoulder. "Ross and the underwriters can look at it later," he said. "Let's get a coffee." He didn't understand why Charles was so worried. EWB had paid the chunky premium weeks ago. Davey had no intention of denying their claim.

The lift to the seventeenth floor was crowded, and, as usual, hushed. Confidentiality precluded business talk, and British reticence stopped conversation about anything else. Marty was relieved when he and Charles were alone in Saxton Brown's serviced offices. He dialled the strongest setting on their state-of-the-art coffee machine and made them both a latte. "What's really the matter, Charles?" he asked.

Charles sipped the drink. "Amy's boss, Marty Bridges, was in business in Bazakistan," he said. "He's been kidnapped. I suspect it's the same bandits who have Ross' fiancée. There's a photograph of poor Marty in chains. It was emailed from his phone. It's too similar to be a coincidence."

"Either that, or Bazakistan's a kidnappers' paradise," Davey said. "I don't recall the Foreign Office giving any warnings, though."

"There couldn't possibly have been any," Charles said. "Ross assesses our product risk and pricing. There's no way he'd have allowed Kat to travel there if he'd really thought for a minute it was that dangerous."

The IT director still looked tense. Davey contemplated, and discounted, the bottle of bourbon. It was too early for anyone to start drinking. "What do the kidnappers want?" he asked.

"Twenty million dollars," Charles said gloomily.

Davey nearly fell off his chair. There couldn't be two greedy sets of kidnappers, both using the same tactics, in a backwater like Bazakistan.

"This is going to cause problems with Ross," Charles said, putting words to the concerns that had started to coalesce in Davey's mind. "We'll get negotiators in to help with Amy's boss, won't we? We have to get him out." He looked anxiously at Davey, as if willing him to agree.

Davey grunted. He needed to examine the claim, and the policy paperwork, carefully. It was pointless to commit to further action until he'd checked the claim was valid.

"But Ross will be on his own," Charles added. "Nobody's helping him negotiate with the kidnappers, or giving him the cash to pay Kat's

93

ransom. If he can't do what those thugs want, Kat may not come home alive."

"I'm sorry," Davey said. "We can't deal with Kat's ransom demand too. It would be completely unethical. Ross didn't buy insurance for her, and we can't use the company's assets to support him, however sympathetic we are." He couldn't afford to be swayed by Charles, or indeed listen to his own emotions. It was going to be a difficult sell to his shareholders as it was. He wasn't looking forward to telling them that the low risk, high margin kidnap insurance business was about to pay twenty million dollars for Amy's boss. Although Ross had undoubtedly passed on some of the risk to the Lloyds market, the company must have retained a proportion itself. Charles' sales victory was looking increasingly hollow.

Ross wasn't in the office, and Davey wondered if he would turn up at all. In Ross' shoes, Davey thought, whether he had flu or not, he'd take leave from work. Ross should be liquidating his assets and speaking to his Bazaki lawyer. Davey was about to ring the actuary to suggest it, when Ross arrived at the office, his face drawn.

"It's not just Kat who's been kidnapped, is it?" he said. "Erik tells me his business partner has disappeared in Bazakistan too." He shook his head. "My future brother-in-law bent my ear for what felt like hours. He's not amused that Kat went there at all, let alone without me. He's even less impressed that he found out via your daughter." He glared at Charles. "Why can't Amy stay out of this?"

Charles looked stunned. "I don't think she did anything wrong," he said, his tone injured.

"The kidnappers want secrecy," Ross said. An air of desperation clung to the young man.

"I'll deal with this," Davey said, noting how Ross was shivering, his eyes sunken and rimmed with dark circles. "I'm sure it's time for your next cigarette, Charles."

"Too right," Charles said, heading for the door. He, too, obviously realised Ross hadn't slept a wink.

"Ross, we'll manage without you for once. Go home, talk to your Bazaki contacts, then try to get some rest," Davey urged. Satisfied the actuary had listened, he took a deep breath, preparing for a meticulous investigation into the new claim.

Chapter 22 **Marty**

A new morning dawned. Marty had slept well. He had more energy this morning, and was glad he'd eaten last night. Rolling over to look at Kat, he watched her green eyes blink open, as if a jeweller had swept back curtains to reveal twin circles of jade.

She yawned and stretched. "I'll be using the bucket," she said, throwing off her blanket.

He made a show of covering his eyes with his hands. It was the least he could to preserve her dignity. She'd do the same for him.

"When we met at Heathrow, I bet you didn't think we'd be sharing a room," he said. He could hear she'd finished, so he risked a wink.

"It wasn't my choice either," Kat replied. "We don't have to see each other again if we get out alive." Her lip trembled.

"When, not if. We'll be free soon," he said, with more confidence than he felt. His helplessness was a bitter pill for a man accustomed to controlling his own destiny and that of others. This bothered him more than the fear lurking in the corners of his mind, banished there by sheer willpower. He forced himself to stay positive for his own sake, for Kat, and for the family and employees who depended on him. "Mr Millionaire will pay up. So will our friends at Saxton Brown. It won't stop me returning to Bazakistan."

"You won't need to," she snapped. The rich stew had obviously restored her strength and brought her old fire back. "I'm reclaiming the vodka factory from that old thief, Aliyev. There'll be no point in you travelling to Kireniat, because you won't be welcome at Snow Mountain."

Harry would have plenty to say about that. Marty knew the engineer wasn't giving up his factory without a fight. Did Ross and Kat imagine they could outspend Harry and his powerful friends? They didn't stand a chance, especially if Ross had to pay a hefty price for her release.

He wondered why Kat wanted the distillery anyway. Amy had told Marty about Kat's partying, her love of dancing and designer dresses. Kireniat was hardly exciting enough for a London socialite. "I don't know why you care about it so much," he said.

"These are my roots," she replied.

Marty groaned in disbelief. "How far back?" he asked. He tried to sweep an arm around the room, forgetting his shackles. The chains clanked. "Look around you. Look especially at the freedom fighters. They're ethnic Bazaki. How long do you think the Russians have been here? I'd guess your parents were shipped out by Stalin. Maybe they were toddlers at the time. Your father ran a factory producing liquor for the Communist USSR. There were no generations toiling in the mountains, lovingly handcrafting vodka for Bazaki aristocrats. There were no aristocrats. No point being misty-eyed about Snow Mountain, bab."

"Still," she persisted, somewhat sulkily. "It's a family tradition, even if just for a generation. My father made Snow Mountain great. He expected me to take on the factory when I grew up. Erik wasn't interested."

Marty could believe her last statement. Erik had always shown an aptitude for science. He was a dreamer too, like his father. Of course, Sasha had been an able engineer and a reasonable manager, but it was Maria who had been the practical one. She'd immediately seen the commercial possibilities when Marty first showed up at the factory. She and Sasha were a good team. Why would she have anything to do with a snake like Aliyev? He shook his head.

Kat misinterpreted the gesture. "I suppose you think a woman can't run a distillery?" she said hotly. "You're wrong. I went to the factory every day in the summer holidays, helping with labels on the bottling line, learning how to produce vodka from start to finish."

That implied scant regard for health and safety, Marty thought wryly, not that it had done her any harm. This wasn't the UK after all, stuck with all that government red tape. He let her continue.

"It was going to be my business one day," Kat said. "The distribution as well. My father intended me to do it when you retired. That's why he sent me to school in England."

"News to me, bab," Marty said. Sasha hadn't breathed a word of it to him, and he would have received a robust response if he had. "I'm passing my business on to my children when I ride into the sunset. I already employ three of them at East West Bridges. My succession planning's sorted."

She gawped at him. Marty could almost see the wheels turning in her head, telling her he was a liar, and it wasn't fair.

There was a sudden crashing sound from the yard, and the door rattled.

"What was that?" Kat nearly leaped out of her skin.

96

Marty looked out of the window. He saw Anna cursing, food and crockery scattered on the ground. A couple of pigs were making a start on the apples.

"Room service is delayed this morning," he said.

Anna recovered quickly enough to appear ten minutes later with a full tray. "No Ken," she said, giving Marty the evil eye before slamming the door behind her.

Once they'd split the bread and apples, Kat was still apparently spoiling for a fight. "You say you're involving your children in your work. Why wouldn't my father do the same for me? I can't believe he didn't tell you."

Marty bit into his apple, savouring the juice. It would be many hours before he ate again. Meanwhile, he'd be cooped up with Kat. He wished she was less agitated. "Calm down," he said gently. "Maybe Sasha never got round to divulging his plans to me. There's much more to Snow Mountain than you realise, though. It isn't just about making vodka. You have to meet regulations for sale, advertising and quality. Taxes have to be paid as you transport and sell the product." He didn't mention the bribes, although judiciously paid commissions were also a fact of life. That was a criminal act back home, so the less Kat knew of it, the better. "Those are the technical aspects. Then the magic starts. You have to build a brand, and protect it. Do you think Sasha did all that?" He didn't wait for her to reply. "No. I registered the Snow Mountain trademark, and my company owns it."

"EWB Ltd belongs to you, then?" Kat asked, biting her lip.

"Correct," Marty said.

"You stole the trademark from my father," she flared.

"No, I listened to my lawyer," Marty said patiently. "Katherine persuaded me to register the brand everywhere I might want to sell it and in many countries I wouldn't. Sasha just wanted the rights in Bazakistan, so he could manufacture within the law. Everywhere else, it's mine. My intellectual property protection is watertight."

"So what?" Kat said, her cheeks flushed. "This is the best vodka in the world, made with water drawn from the mountains. Without it, your trademark's a worthless piece of paper."

"I could make Snow Mountain vodka anywhere in the world," Marty said mildly. "Birmingham, for example." After all, he owned enough land and old buildings to set up a factory there.

"Birmingham versus Bazakistan?" she said, her derision audible. "Scarcely the same cachet."

"Not for London, it's true," Marty admitted. "It would do very well in Brum itself." The city was proud of its successes, it was well-endowed with upmarket cocktail bars and pubs, and he had an excellent local business network. "I tell you what would work, though, Kat. A distillery in the Welsh mountains. That would play well in London, and actually, I'd get great sales in cities like Paris where they don't love the English." He almost forgot his parlous situation as he began to daydream. A Welsh holiday cottage would suit him, a bolthole where he could tinker with the classic cars and motorbikes that annoyed Angela so much.

He became aware that Kat was looking unimpressed. "I made that brand," he said. "When I arrived in Kireniat on my motorbike, I found a barely functioning vodka factory. Kireniat was a ghost town. It was the Wild East out here."

"What do you mean?" she asked. "We weren't living in mud huts."

"Kireniat was a crazy place," he said. "It wasn't the cosmopolitan city it is today. The Soviet Union had disintegrated and Bazakistan was independent. Your countrymen were excited about that, but it came at a price. The old state-organised distribution chains had broken down. Everywhere I went, there were shortages. Only three things were abundant: land, people and vodka."

She'd been a baby then. How could she possibly remember, and how could be begin to explain?

"I knew the fall of the Soviet Union would bring opportunities," he said. "I taught myself Russian in three months and started importing vodka from Russia in a small way. My name was known within the trade. Your father heard of me through the grapevine."

"He made a big mistake choosing you as his distributor," Kat said. "He must have had salesmen queueing up to buy his product."

Marty ignored the slur. "No chance," he said. "When I first met him, your father was making vodka from any raw materials he could find. He would have made it from old shoes if he could have got enough of them. Under Communism, the factory's targets were based purely on quantity, not quality. Sasha wanted to change that, but first he had to find money to keep the factory going. He was desperate. Nobody would do anything for him without a bribe, not even supply electricity."

"I bet you took advantage of that," Kat said.

"Hardly," Marty said. "The stuff he made was so rough, I'd have been mad to buy it. But Sasha convinced me he could make a quality product, and I handed over a down-payment. I didn't rip him off. I wanted a long term relationship."

Kat snorted.

"You don't know how lucky your family was," Marty said. "Sasha had sent telexes to every Western vodka distributor he could. None of them replied. It was hardly surprising, you know. In the West, we were already using faxes, perhaps the odd email." It was lucky that Angela, then his secretary, liked the telex machine.

"Not only that, Kat. Did Sasha ever tell you how hard it was to get to Bazakistan in those days?" Marty continued. "Bazakair was the only airline allowed to land at Kireniat, and it made up its flight schedules as it went along. It couldn't always afford fuel, even when it coaxed its decrepit kites into the air."

"How did you get here, then?" Kat asked.

Marty grinned, remembering his big adventure. "On a motorbike."

In polite, painstaking English, Sasha's telexes had told him to travel by train from Istanbul, then buy a motorbike at a car auction two hundred miles from Kireniat. He should bring plenty of dollars for police bribes, food and fuel – and to buy vodka when he reached his destination.

"I picked up, of all things, an old Triumph Bonneville," Marty said.

Kat looked blank.

"It was made in the Midlands," he said. "I've no idea how it ended up here."

The journey hadn't been without danger. Although a keen boxer in his youth, his fists weren't proof against knives. Marty had protected himself by carrying one, and knowing how to use it. A can of pepper spray was handy too.

Riding along the rocky, pitted highways, resting in farms rather than towns, he stayed safe and retained his possessions. He probably ate better as well. Food was expensive in urban areas, and in short supply.

"I arrived at the Kireniat Number Three Vodka Factory with a Russian phrasebook in one hand and a fistful of dollars in the other. And then the fun started."

Fortunately, Sasha was forward-thinking. He'd listened as Marty explained that the West required a high-quality product, with an air of mystique and exclusivity. They'd decided to use only the best wheat, and capitalise on the crystal-clear stream that flowed past the factory from the mountains. Viewing the snowy crags beyond Kireniat, Marty had christened the brand.

"Once Sasha and I had ironed out the quality issues, I designed the label," Marty said. He was proud of it, a simple line drawing of jagged peaks tipped with snow. "I registered the Snow Mountain trademark. I devised the marketing strategy. High end outlets only. I didn't need a degree like your friend, Amy." He didn't care if Kat was listening. He was on a roll. "It wasn't easy at first. I paid a fortune to airlift consignments out of Bazakistan. There was no other way. I sent food parcels, too, for Sasha to feed his family – you – and his workforce."

He'd despatched what seemed like half the EU food mountain to Bazakistan. Fortunately, after a few years, the transition to capitalism was complete and the country's fuel and food shortages eased. Then, Sasha could use trusted lorry drivers equipped with dollars to grease official palms. That was when they really started to make money.

"So don't think Snow Mountain is just about you and your family," Marty said. "I have a massive stake in it too."

"I know." Kat scowled at him. "A stake you weren't willing to give up when my father was thrown into prison. You could have threatened to walk away and take all that marketing know-how with you."

"What makes you think I didn't?" Marty asked. "I spent a fortune on lawyers' fees and commissions too, without success." Nothing had worked. He'd just had to accept the new reality: that Sasha was in prison and Harry owned the factory.

Kat pursed her lips. "An honourable man would have left Aliyev to flounder."

Marty shook his head. "I wanted to secure your father's release. I had to co-operate with Harry." By the time Sasha died, it was evident that, although Marty disliked and distrusted Harry, he could do business with the man. Like Sasha, Harry listened. Together, they'd taken the brand global. It was respected, requested and served in the finest establishments in half the world's capitals.

Kat's face darkened further. "I know it isn't about my family," she said, "at least, not where you're concerned. For you, it's all about profit, cash in your bank account. You can't take it with you, old man. I hope the rebels kill you. Because when you could have saved my father and mother, you counted your money and did nothing."

Chapter 23 Davey

Davey's troubles diminished and his excitement rose as he neared the glossy black door. Had his life been free of the family responsibilities that were rapidly losing their charm, he would have liked to live in the flat Dee had shared with Charles. The Mayfair garden square was the epitome of understated opulence, its four sides lined with the white, iron-balconied houses that most Londoners adored and few could afford.

As usual, the Saxton Brown CEO looked around, satisfying himself he didn't know any of the passers-by who sauntered past, oblivious to Davey and his plans for the evening. The location was sufficiently far from the City to render this unlikely. He unlocked the door, noting there was now a large placard on the balcony railings announcing "Milsom Painters & Decorators" were working there.

Inside the first floor apartment, the scale of the renovations became apparent. Dustsheets covered the cream carpets and there was a strong smell of paint. Davey was about to call Alana to suggest they rented a hotel room instead, when he noticed the time. She'd be here in ten minutes.

Quickly, he checked the drinks cabinet. The bourbon he'd left was untouched by Milsom and his men, as was a bottle of champagne. Davey slipped it in the fridge with the food he'd bought to eat later.

He'd had a trying day, with Ross and Charles both on edge, and he suspected Alana had too. There were rumours in the City that Bishopstoke's profits were down, and their investors restless for change. She'd need cheering up. He no longer resented her for beating him to the top job in the merged company; their love affair had taken away the sting of losing that competition. A leer played on Davey's lips as he recalled how Alana had wanted him so much, she'd deliberately pumped Dee for information about him before that magical night in Birmingham.

Davey undressed. He was wearing just a towel and a broad smile when he buzzed Alana into the flat. Barely hesitating to close the door, he flung the scrap of cloth to one side, enveloping her in his embrace.

She surrendered willingly. "You're so fit," she said, pinching his firm biceps.

Davey smirked, gratified at the adoring look in her eyes. "The Iron Man's getting closer," he said. He could feel his endurance improve. For over an hour, he kept time to the beat of his favourite metal tracks.

"Do you want to stay?" he asked afterwards. "I can cook for you."

She nodded, pulling on her business suit.

Davey dressed, then opened the bottle of champagne, filling two flutes. "Cheers," he said.

"Cheers." Alana downed the fizz. "That's cleared my head," she said. "What's for dinner?"

"A surprise," Davey said. "Ready in five minutes."

"Proof you can microwave a ready meal," Alana said, with a knowing grin. "I'd have done the same myself if I'd returned home before dinner. Home cooking is for wimps."

Laura would have candles and flowers on the table, and a stew bubbling on the hob. Davey banished the thought as he busied himself in the kitchen. An acceptable beef stroganoff appeared almost instantly.

"Thank you." Alana smiled. "How's business?"

He was surprised she'd asked, although it gave him permission to discuss Bishopstoke's plight and offer sympathy. "Up and down," he said.

"Oh." Alana seemed taken aback. She recovered enough to say, "It's the same at Bishopstoke."

"I heard," Davey said. "The City of London is a hard taskmaster. Commiserations."

"I've had our merchant bankers threaten blood in the boardroom," Alana said. She pushed the carb-heavy rice to the side of her plate, stabbing a strip of steak with her fork. "I tell you, there will be plenty of blood if I find out who leaked our results. And it won't be mine." There was a vicious glint in her eyes.

"Let me guess," Davey said. "They want more exciting insurance products, with fatter profit margins." It was a well-worn refrain he'd heard from investors for years. Fortunately, he was delivering it, although Marty's kidnap would dent Saxton Brown's profits.

"Exactly," Alana said. "I'm finding my finance director is useless. I thought accountants were supposed to be creative. He's only interested in adding up the group's profits, when I need him to find a way to make them look bigger."

Davey suspected she'd be disappointed. New financial regulations had removed most opportunities to massage accounts numbers. He cleared their plates away. "How about chocolate mousse?" he asked.

"There's only one way chocolate passes my lips," Alana said.

He recalled their first night together. "Later, then," he teased.

"Yes, we still need to talk business," Alana said. "You've got interesting niche products at Saxton Brown. Your kidnap, key man and business interruption insurance books, to name three. I could do great things with them at Bishopstoke. Sell them to me, Davey."

He was flabbergasted. "Not now, sweetheart," he said, taking her hand in his. "I've told you before they're not up for sale."

Alana pulled her hand away. "You don't understand. I really need this. I'm prepared to make an offer you can't refuse."

"But I will refuse," Davey said, sighing. "Don't spoil a fun evening, Alana." He stroked her face.

She kissed his lips lightly, and simpered. "You'd do it if you cared about me," she said.

He ignored the desire that flared within him. What was her angle? He'd made it clear at the start of their relationship that his business was out of bounds to her. "Don't try emotional blackmail," he said, forcing a chuckle, reluctant to show her she'd rattled him.

"I'm not joking," Alana said. She pouted. "Too bad if you don't care about me. What about your wife? How would you like her to know about us?"

"She doesn't need to," Davey said, alarmed.

"Indulge me, and she won't," Alana said. "Sell me the business. I can have my lawyers write up terms tomorrow."

Her implacable gaze worried him. He understood she wanted to save her job, but she was going too far. "You're kidding," he said. "You can't prove anything."

"Oh no?" Alana said. "I suppose I haven't seen that little mole on your left buttock. And..." She proceeded to list every pimple, blemish and physical imperfection on his body.

The music stopped as Davey squirmed, horrified. It was obvious that Alana need only pick up the phone to his wife. To his dismay, he was certain she'd do it if he continued to resist. He faced an invidious choice: to lose either his marriage, or Saxton Brown, the company he'd worked so hard to build.

103

"My lawyers will call you tomorrow, baby," she said, blowing him a kiss. "Ciao."

Chapter 24 **Davey**

"Why are you selling half of our business?" Charles asked. "I don't get it."

Davey looked at the ceiling. After a sleepless night, he'd reached a decision. He was proud to have taken Saxton Brown from a mere twinkle in his eye to a successful company. While it was important to him, his marriage meant much more. Laura wasn't just the mother of his children, but his soulmate. If Saxton Brown must be sacrificed to keep her, he'd do it.

He could hardly tell Charles the truth. "There's Marty's kidnap, Charles," he said. "It's an outlier, at the highest end of the spectrum of potential claims. A catastrophe, you could say. There will be a large hole in our capital should we have to pay it all. We haven't yet built a big enough book to spread our risk."

Charles winced. "Alana Green will never give you full value when there's a large claim outstanding, though, will she? She's got an aggressive reputation – and from what I've seen, it's well-deserved."

"She knows what she wants," Davey said.

Ross, silent until now, chipped in. He was nursing a large black coffee and had bags under his eyes. "Tell Alana you won't sell," he said. "And tell the kidnappers you won't pay." His blue eyes glittered and his fists clenched. He looked dangerous, ready for a fight. "That's what I've done. I've emailed them to say there are plenty of beautiful girls in Bazakistan. I can get another one any time I like." He shook his head. "I'm calling their bluff, Davey. You should play poker, like I do. It's excellent training for life."

Charles put his head in his hands.

Davey, too, was taken aback. "Not this time," he said. The thought crossed his mind that Kat's brother was right to despise Ross as a potential brother-in-law. He doubted that Angela Bridges, or indeed any of their wealthy clients, would appreciate the company treating an insurance claim like a hand of poker.

The days of good-natured banter with his team seemed a lifetime away. Thinking longingly of his old office overlooking the Thames, now occupied by Alana, he found a quiet corner and called her. She scarcely bothered to keep the note of triumph from her voice as she told him her consultants would be round at twelve. Naturally, she wanted a team to perform due diligence on the business.

Although the process would take several weeks, Alana's consultants arrived armed with a list of initial questions. Davey answered them all in two hours over coffee and sandwiches. He wasn't surprised to receive a call from Alana later that day.

"You know that kidnap claim? My guys say material facts weren't disclosed. Put it on hold," she instructed him.

Davey glanced at Charles: drinking buddy, baby George's father, and committed IT director. He was so committed to Saxton Brown, in fact, that he'd sold kidnap insurance to his daughter's boss. Like all their clients, Marty had paid the premiums believing that if he encountered problems, Saxton Brown would be on his side. Marty's family and friends desperately wanted the Brummie businessman rescued from Bazakistan. So did Charles. They all had a right to expect Davey to do everything in his power to achieve it. How, in all conscience, could Davey put Marty's life at risk by declining either to pay the ransom or negotiate with the kidnappers? "I can't do that, Alana," he said.

She launched into a tirade. The claim stank. It was outrageously high, out of all proportion to the premium paid. Bazakistan was a stable country with an excellent record on law enforcement. Even the British Foreign Office acknowledged that. The claimant, a friend of Davey's IT director, was a businessman who frequently visited Bazakistan and had never been kidnapped before. Why, no similar crimes had been reported in Bazakistan for decades.

"That's not true at all," Davey said, spotting the kitchenette was empty and making a beeline for it so Charles wouldn't overhear him. "My chief actuary's girlfriend has been kidnapped as well."

Alana sounded exasperated. "Can't you see it's a fraud?" she said. "You should kick his sorry ass out of your company, and that IT director too. They're taking you for a ride."

Davey's hackles rose. The notion was risible. "I'll run Saxton Brown exactly as I wish," he said stiffly.

Alana's response was icy. "We can do this the hard way if you want. I'll take account of it in the price," she said. "Why, you'll be paying me to take the business away. What will your shareholders say? Or the City institutions when they hear it's so easy to make a fool of you?"

106

She'd made a fool of him already, he thought. Aloud, he said, "The Ombudsman would skin me alive."

Alana laughed. "I'll take care of the Ombudsman. I have my methods."

Davey had no doubt on that score.

Chapter 25 **Kat**

It had been a week, chained in a poky room with Marty Bridges. Kat was exhausted and unsettled. Since the drugs were withdrawn, she'd struggled to sleep, painfully aware of her chains and Marty's unwanted company. She yearned, yet failed, to blot out her discomfort and fear.

Their conditions had marginally improved once the rebels' leader finally returned to the farm. This was the man they called Ken, the only one who spoke English well. Marty, who spent hours by the narrow window listening to their captors' small talk, said Ken appeared to stay in a number of safe houses. Upon spying the man's silver Mercedes, Marty had immediately hollered for him.

Kat had listened as Marty compared their cell with a dog kennel, then complained there was no need to drug the captives; as they were both chained, the worst action they could take was overturning the bucket of excrement. A dirty protest was hardly going to make their lives more pleasant, so why would they do it? In fact, the hostages needed washing facilities, and soon. If Ken wanted to be President one day, this treatment was scarcely guaranteed to win over foreign investors.

Kat had formed the impression that Ken was barely interested. He'd growled that the sooner he was paid and rid of them, the better. Nevertheless, another bucket, with lukewarm water, was brought at once. Towels were provided. Kat and Marty averted their eyes from each other and washed as best they could.

Now their twice-daily meals weren't drugged, she had more energy, but no outlet for it. Her resentment at Marty's collaboration with Aliyev continued to simmer as she paced the cell. Between them, they'd stolen her father's business, as well as his life. Even if she survived her captivity, what awaited her afterwards? Was it the soulless existence of a trophy wife? She shuddered. It was better than the alternative: abandonment by Ross, to die at Ken's hands. Why hadn't her fiancé bought her freedom yet?

The boredom and terror of her plight, and the aggravation of sharing it with Marty, were oppressive in spite of his attempts to introduce levity. At his prompting, they played I Spy, fantasy bathroom and fantasy restaurant.

"What's your perfect dinner party, bab?" Marty asked. "Let's pretend. Who would you invite?"

Kat made a charade of considering it. "Ross," she said. "And Prince Harry. Maybe Jamie Dornan."

"To keep Ross on his toes?" Marty grinned.

"You said it," Kat replied. Despite her distaste for him, he could make her laugh.

"You can invite women too," Marty suggested. "Especially if they're plain. Then they can't outshine you."

She gave him such a filthy look that he backtracked. "Nobody could outshine you, Kat," he added.

"I'll ask Dame Vivienne Westwood," she said. "And Adele. They're both interesting, but definitely not Ross' type. Do the guests have to be real people, anyway?"

"Hold on," Marty said, mock horror on his face. "Before you move to the realms of fiction, aren't you forgetting someone? What about me?"

Didn't he realise that she still wouldn't choose to spend a minute with him in the absence of their chains? "You're not on the guest list," she told him.

"I'd be your wine waiter," he said, "if only to get close to Adele."

That poor secretary he'd married – Angela, wasn't it? – might have a view on that. "No," Kat said. "We'll dine at the Dorchester." The hotel name was plucked from thin air. "They don't need any staff."

"And what culinary delights await you?" Marty asked, unabashed.

"Caviar and quails' eggs on toast," Kat said. "Beef Wellington with roast potatoes and asparagus. Death by chocolate, strawberries, and lashings of champagne." Her mouth watered. The menu would be most acceptable for a wedding breakfast as well.

"I'm afraid the Dorchester is fully booked this week, Madam," Marty said. "However, tonight I can give you a reservation at the Hotel California. Your host: that Mercedes-driving revolutionary himself, Mr Ken Khan. The chef: Miss Anna, horsemeat stew a speciality. Best of all, you may share a floor for two with your old pal, Marty Bridges. You're not going to turn down an offer like that, are you?"

She pulled a face, blinking tears from her eyes. Marty noticed and put his arms around her as far as his shackles would permit. That was worse. Kat shrank from him. She knew he meant to comfort her, but his touch had quite the opposite effect. She wished she was alone. Marty's presence was part of the problem.

Anna didn't bring the evening meal today. Kat could hear the girl outside, muttering with annoyance. Their waiter for the evening was Ulan.

He was younger than the others, barely into his twenties at a guess. His black hair was spiky, very short, like a soldier's. Although there was usually a wide grin on his chunky, amiable face, Kat disliked him more than her other captors. His sly glances had begun to set alarm bells ringing. As he brought in the tray with stew, bread and apples, he leered at her.

"Good evening, Ulan," Marty said, his voice icy with mistrust.

Kat turned her back on the Bazaki, still feeling the heat of his gaze until the door slammed and she and Marty were alone.

"Creepy, isn't he?" Marty said. "I'd lock up my daughters if I saw him on the prowl." He stuck a spoon in his bowl. "I'll give you odds of two to one this is the latest recipe from Anna's equine cookbook. It's a racing certainty."

Although Kat shared his suspicions about the provenance of the meat, the stew both smelled and tasted appetising. There were dumplings and herbs in the rich, savoury mixture. She ate heartily.

"You can't beat a good cuppa," Marty said, gulping the sweet tea. He stretched and yawned.

Kat felt overcome by fatigue herself. The tedium of the setting only served to amplify it. Nothing would happen this evening, except perhaps a game of fantasy cocktail bar, as if she and Marty were small children dreaming in a playground. Soon, daylight would begin to dim. Ulan would remove the tray and, if they were lucky, clean the slops bucket. She would be left with Marty, the impossible hope of recovering Snow Mountain, and the growing fear that she wouldn't leave Bazakistan alive. Ross might not have enough cash for the kidnappers, or fail to raise it in time. He could even meet another girl. It was well known that Kireniat was blessed with alluring maidens chasing foreign husbands, and he didn't even need to go as far as Bazakistan. London was full of beautiful single females like Kat herself.

Her eyelids drooped. Better, she felt, to fall asleep than drive herself mad worrying about Ross' infidelity. She lay on the pile of rugs and blankets that served as a mattress, staring across the room at the sputtering stove. Their gaolers tended to throw the odd log into it, keeping the fire alive without causing it to blaze. There was little imperative to heat the cell now the snow had gone and spring had suddenly arrived.

She willed herself into a trance, letting sleep claim her. It was dark when she awoke. The dim glow of moonlight through the window outlined a man standing in front of her.

"Marty?" she said, and found the effort of speaking was almost too much. It wasn't Marty either, she realised with dread. He was slumped under a blanket a few yards away, his snores echoing through the small space.

The man knelt down, his face closer but still a gloomy shadow. Moonlight cast a halo around his close-cropped, spiky hair. She smelled sweat, tobacco and alcohol. Then the shadow moved, and its mouth was on hers, roughly kissing her lips.

It had to be Ulan. As he threw off her blanket, his hands pawing at her clothes to undo buttons and zips, she tried to punch and kick. Her arms and legs remained strangely immobile, weighed down by her chains.

Briefly, he stopped kissing her, to draw breath.

"No," she shouted, first in English, then Russian.

Ulan laughed. "You are beautiful girl," he said, slipping his fingers under her blouse and grabbing a handful of flesh.

He twisted her nipple. An involuntary wave of pleasure surged through her, and she retched, gagging. She desperately wanted to struggle and was completely unable to. As he brought his mouth to hers again, his stubble scratching her face, she summoned the energy to scream.

The emerging sound was muffled by Ulan's kiss, but it had an effect. Marty awoke.

"What?" he said, his voice slurred.

With a heavy heart, Kat finally understood. Ulan had reneged on Ken Khan's promise. They'd both been drugged.

Marty evidently was alert enough to comprehend the situation. He pulled himself to a sitting position, grunting with exertion. "Can't stand...up," he said. "Stop."

Ulan jeered at him in Russian. "You're wasting your time," he said. "This woman's worthless, to us and to you. No one will pay anything for her. You may as well have your fun after I've had mine."

Kat screamed, a wail of despair, terror and anger. She put every ounce of her being into resisting Ulan as he parted her legs. It wasn't enough.

The youth easily spread-eagled them either side of him, unbuckling his jeans, panting with excitement.

Unable to stand, Marty found the strength to roll into them both, knocking Ulan to the ground. At the same time, Anna and Ken's voices could be heard outside. The door rattled and shook. It was locked.

"Ulan is here." Marty's voice was hoarse and low. Would Ken hear it?

"Open that door," Ken yelled.

Ulan scrambled to his feet. He unlocked the door. "I was just checking up on them," he said, his tone sullen.

The beam of Ken's torch swept every corner of the room. His eyes narrowed as he took in Kat's dishevelled appearance and Marty's grogginess. "Is this true?" he asked.

"No," Marty said slowly. "It was a rape attempt."

"What have I told you?" Ken raged at Ulan.

"Her boyfriend's refused to pay, hasn't he? What use is she to you?" Ulan said resentfully.

"She is still our guest. They both are. We must treat them accordingly," Ken said.

"Guests?" Marty muttered, looking pointedly at his chains as Ulan cowered under Ken's glare.

"You speak a little Russian?" Ken said. "I wish to show you hospitality, Marty, but we must take sensible precautions." He glowered at Ulan. "Clearly, that applies to my team as well. I can only apologise. It won't happen again." He stormed out, Anna and Ulan trailing after him. The lock turned.

Was it true that Ross had refused to pay anything? Kat shivered. If Ken didn't expect to receive a ransom for her, why wasn't she dead? Ken seemed to regard the hostages as an inconvenience at best; surely he wouldn't keep her alive as an act of charity? She sniffed, but still, the tears began and continued to fall.

"Bab?" Marty's voice sounded distant, but sympathetic. "Are you all right?"

"No," she said. Grasping how much worse her predicament would have been if he hadn't defended her earlier, she added, "but thank you." Her lips and tongue felt thick. The words were barely intelligible.

"Don't mention it," Marty slurred. "Try to sleep."

"Marty," she said. She was beginning to think she'd misjudged him. "I could work with you after all."

112

Marty yawned. He couldn't quite manage a chortle. "Bab, what makes you think I'd want to work with you?" he said.

Kat was still formulating her reply when they heard the single gunshot.

Chapter 26 **Marty**

Only Anna, Nurbolat and a youth Marty didn't know appeared the morning after the gunshot. They seemed subdued, rarely speaking except to mumble when they stopped for a cigarette. Marty caught very little of their conversation as he listened at the window.

Kat's mental health gave him cause for concern. Mostly, she sat huddled in a blanket, refusing even to pick at the food Anna brought. A few sips of tea were all she permitted herself. Marty saved bread and apples in case she changed her mind later.

"Cheer up, it may never happen," he said. At least that provoked a glare.

He opened the window, and closed it in a hurry. The wind was blowing from the direction of Anna's pigsty. He'd seen her pigs and chickens scurrying around the yard, apparently content to eat muddy weeds and worse. Was it really worth paying a premium for free-range food, he wondered? His wife seemed to think so. He mused fondly on Angela's idiosyncrasies: the diets he tried to subvert, and her belief, which he'd often derided, that he should retire and take her on a cruise around the world. Perhaps he would if he left this hell-hole alive.

"When," he said. "Not if, when."

Kat stirred. "I beg your pardon?" she said.

"We'll get out of here, Kat," he told her.

"You have a plan?" she said, her face brightening at last.

"Not yet," he admitted, relieved that she was showing signs of animation. "But," he added, smiling with a confidence that he didn't feel, "leave it to me and I'll think of one. And I don't care how many of the bastards I have to kill." The risk to their lives – and to Kat's sanity – was too great otherwise. Ken was overly trigger-happy, his minions thuggish.

"Their hearts are in the right place," Kat said, to his astonishment.

"Oh really?" Marty said. "These filthy animals drug us, chain us, throw us in a cell, try to rape you, put us in fear of our lives and doubtless make our nearest and dearest sick with worry – but they're just cuddly pussycats after all? Whatever they stuck in the stew last night, you're still hallucinating from it."

"I know they've treated us badly. But you said Ken wanted to bring down the President," she said. "It needs to be done. If they hadn't behaved so callously," she trembled, clearly remembering the events of the previous evening, "I might have joined them."

His mouth gaped. "You can't be serious," he protested. "This is Stockholm Syndrome. You've been brainwashed. How have they managed it? You've only been here a week."

"No," Kat said. Her eyes flashed. "The President's an evil old man. While you played a part in my parents' deaths, he was even more culpable. He gave the order."

Marty groaned. When would she believe he'd done everything he could? He just had to accept Kat would never be his best friend.

"You flatter yourself and your family," he said. "What makes you think the President even knew who Sasha was?" It was harsh, but the truth as he saw it. "More likely, Kat – far more likely – your troubles stem from some nameless, faceless petty official whom Sasha failed to bribe." Sadly, it was probably more prosaic than that. He suspected Harry Aliyev's dirty hand on the knife. Harry, jealous of Sasha's material success and coveting his attractive wife, paying backhanders to have his boss thrown into prison. Sasha's death two years later was most convenient for Harry, enabling him to acquire the grieving widow as well as the vodka factory. Who knew how much Harry had paid for that?

He might be wrong about Marina Aliyeva, of course. As Marty glanced at Kat, he didn't think so. It gave him no pleasure to know Harry had been cuckolded for his troubles. His face darkened. He turned away from Kat and walked to the window, looking out intently, screwing up his eyes, using all his willpower to stave off tears.

Chapter 27 **Ken**

"You didn't kill him," Marina said, her lips pursed with displeasure.

"How do you know?" Ken asked, playing for time. He sipped his latte.

"Arystan tells me Marty Bridges has been kidnapped," she said. "A huge ransom has been demanded. Not that you'd know it, from the newspapers or TV. There's nothing about it online, even."

Ken was relieved to hear it. His increasingly intemperate ransom demands had threatened dire consequences if the authorities were informed, but he couldn't be sure his desire for secrecy would prevail. Of course, there was still a risk that the Bazaki government was well aware of Marty's predicament, and was simply exercising its customary censorship. "I don't know anything about it," he lied. "Although it explains why I can't find him anywhere."

"Arystan's worried," she said. "He doesn't know anything about marketing, and he thinks he'll have to find another distributor."

"And you?" Ken asked. "What do you think?"

She shrugged. "It's an established brand. Someone else will take it on."

That vodka factory should be nationalised, Ken thought, then the state would benefit from its profits again. Perhaps Marina could run it. Aliyev was in too deep with the dictatorship. There would have to be a trial, naturally, but he'd make sure Aliyev didn't survive the revolution.

Two uniformed policemen entered the coffee bar, AK-47s slung across their bodies. They were professionals, their eyes never still, glancing everywhere. Ken made ready to flee, then relaxed as the men ordered drinks and took them away.

It was unlikely, he knew, that anyone would recognise either him or Marina Aliyeva. He was wearing a woolly hat and dark glasses, as an older man might to hide a bald head and bags under his eyes. She sported sunglasses and a white silk headscarf, tied under her chin. Sometimes, the best place to hide was in a crowd. That was why he'd suggested the Kireniat Mall, the massive shopping centre through which tens of thousands of Bazakis passed every day.

Marina spotted his discomfort. "Shall we go to the hotel?" she asked.

It was part of a local chain, built into the mall. Scores of couples probably arrived here each day with the same purpose in mind. The young male receptionist as good as winked at Ken when Marina handed over a bundle of crisp notes for their room.

"I thought it would be nicer for you here," he said, as they threw themselves down on the big white bed and began kissing.

"I bet the lovely hot showers were attractive too, compared with cold water from a well," Marina observed.

"Is that a hint?" he asked, laughing. "Let's take one together."

She let him strip her, and lead her into the bathroom. It was a white, windowless room that smelled of apples. Again, as he ran his hands over her pale, taut body, he felt himself consumed by the silky warmth of her flesh. She was hungry for him too, nibbling his shoulders in the shower, cupping her hand around his groin. He made her wait until they were back on the bed before entering her. She responded with enthusiasm, writhing backwards and forwards, her skin flushing. When they came in unison, it was the most exquisite sensation he'd ever experienced.

It was never like this with his wife. She'd been a virgin when they met, and was still coy in the bedroom. Ken desperately wanted her back in Bazakistan, but not at the expense of his relationship with Marina. Their passion was too intense. He reassured himself that no one knew. They'd kept their secret until now, and they'd continue to do so in future. They would find a way.

Afterwards, he returned to Starbucks with Kat and Marty's mobile phones. Switching them on, he swiftly sent messages to Arman Khan and Angela Bridges. They would receive body parts if no cash was forthcoming, he told them. In reality, he'd made up his mind. It was too risky to hold hostages any longer. If he released the pair, they'd remember too much about the cars, the orchard and the kidnappers. Even his initial plan, of taking them through the mountains and over the border, was unsafe. They'd be debriefed by the British, their intelligence passed back to the President's men. He didn't want anyone leading the police to his hideout before he'd bought weapons and armed his network of keen young fighters. Tonight, he thought, he would kill his captives quickly. That would please Marina too, and with luck, he'd still receive the ransom.

117

Chapter 28 **Marty**

Anna and Nurbolat appeared to be having an argument.

"I've got to feed the pigs," she said. "Why do we have to go now?"

"Ken says we must collect a freezer and other supplies," Nurbolat replied. He drew a finger across his throat and pointed to the window, seemingly unaware Marty was gazing from it. "You have to come with me. We'll look like a young couple shopping together."

"I want no part in it," Anna said.

The discussion, in Bazaki, became heated. Although Marty couldn't catch all of it, its tenor was unmistakable. Nurbolat was winning.

Moments later, a Mercedes – not the shiny silver model Ken drove, but a battered black car – was driven into the yard. Marty saw Nurbolat at the wheel. Anna opened the passenger door to sit next to him, and the vehicle clattered away.

What did Ken and Nurbolat have in mind? Marty recalled old reports of dead hostages, their bodies frozen and photographed with daily newspapers to pretend they were still alive. It was the cruellest of frauds, giving false hope to bereaved families. There was no point waiting to find out if he was right. He had to act before Nurbolat returned.

The younger man, whom Marty hadn't seen before that morning, remained in the yard. He was tinkering with a motorbike as pop music blared from a wind-up radio. Marty gathered it was the Bazaki hit parade. He called Kat to the window when one of Adele's songs was aired.

"Have you got a plan yet?" Kat asked.

"I might have," Marty said, reluctant to share his fears. He had the barest outline of a plot – to entice the youth inside, trap him and take his keys – but it was better than nothing.

There were risks, he knew. If they failed, they couldn't expect their captor to be merciful. Even if they succeeded, what would happen next? The lad might not be alone on the farm. The smallholding was isolated too; the dirt track was proof of that. How would they escape and what might they find? If they were unlucky, wolves would find them. He'd heard them howling at night. They lived wild in Bazakistan. This wasn't England, where the countryside had been tamed and the largest feral creatures he'd seen were urban foxes at the bottom of his garden.

Marty decided to wait until he knew for sure that the lad had fixed the motorbike. He whispered his ideas to Kat.

For the first time that week, she smiled. He'd evidently thrown her a lifeline. "Let's do it soon," she said. "I don't care about the risks. Remember what Ulan said. I'm as good as dead anyway."

Perhaps they both were, Marty thought. He heard the motorbike engine roar into life outside and told Kat to scream. To Marty's dismay, the boy ignored them, even when the window was opened.

"Shout 'Fire' in Russian," he suggested.

Kat looked puzzled. "I thought we were pretending we didn't know any," she said.

Marty groaned. "It doesn't matter any more," he said. "Ken suspects. And it might be the only way to communicate with our friend."

"Very well." She yelled at the top of her voice, while Marty banged on the door.

"What's the matter?" the youth shouted.

"Fire!" Kat repeated.

They heard the key in the lock. The boy peeped cautiously inside, but he wasn't careful enough. Standing behind the door, Marty sprang out, barging into the young man, sending him sprawling on the floor.

Swiftly, Kat crouched by the lad's head, placing her hands either side of his neck, then taking them behind it. The chain between her wrists wrapped itself around his neck. She pulled it just tight enough to make him gag. "I could kill you in an instant," she threatened in his local tongue. "Give Marty the keys and I might let you go."

"I don't have them," he protested.

She began to garrotte him, while Marty patted down his pockets.

The boy spluttered and lashed out at her. "Enough," Kat commanded, pulling the chain tighter.

It didn't stop the lad. He aimed a vicious kick at Marty, landing a blow to his chest and sending him flying.

"You want to play rough?" Marty said. He had no time for this. Coldly, he stamped on the boy's ribcage.

Winded and in pain, their prisoner stopped struggling. Marty stuffed a corner of a blanket in the youth's mouth to stifle his groans. Finally, he emptied the lad's pockets. "There's nothing apart from this," he said, fishing out a pack of cigarettes and a lighter.

"He must have keys," Kat said. "How else would he get in?"

Marty glanced at the door, seeing the keyring glinting in the afternoon sun. He stepped over the youth's limbs, barely thrashing now, and pulled it from the lock.

"There are several for padlocks," he said. "I'll try your feet first, Kat."

He applied one of the smaller keys to the lock on her ankle chain. It almost clicked. He tried two more before the padlock opened. With a sigh, Kat shook herself free of the heavy chain.

"Now we have a problem," Marty said. "I can remove the shackles from my feet, but not my hands. If I unlocked your hands, you could help me, but you're rather occupied with our friend at the minute."

They both looked at the young man's wrists and ankles, then at each other.

"Okay," Marty said with a grin. He released the chain from his feet, and began trussing the prisoner's ankles with it, finishing by binding and padlocking the lad's feet and hands. "See how you like it," he said.

At last, Marty could unchain Kat's wrists. She returned the favour. They both stretched.

"We have to hit the road," Marty said, locking the youth in their cell. Anxiously, he scanned the yard for signs of life. Apart from birdsong and the clucking of hens, there was none, but for how long? "Ready to start up the bike?" he asked.

Kat laughed, euphoria bringing back her sparkle at last. "Ready as I'll ever be. I've never tried."

"You don't know what you're missing," Marty said. He quickly inspected the motorcycle. "A Ural 650," he mused. It was a Russian brand old enough to be classed as vintage, but appeared to be in good order. Like many elderly machines, there was no fuel gauge. In the past, he'd checked petrol levels by sitting on his bikes and shaking them from side to side, but there was no time for that now. They'd just have to take their chances. Travelling anywhere was safer than staying.

He was prepared to hotwire the bike, but saw its owner had left the key in it. Marty jumped on, turned the key and kicked back with his left foot on the ignition pedal. The engine roared into life as the ignition lever's recoil delivered a thump to his ankle.

Marty cursed, then relented. "Well, the engine's sweet as a nut," he said. "That boy knew what he was doing." He smirked. "As a mechanic, anyway. Hop on the back, Kat. There are no grab handles, so you'll have to hold me tight. Very tight, because that track is as bumpy as any I've seen. It'll be a rough ride."

Kat perched daintily behind him, putting her arms around his abdomen reluctantly.

"This is no time to stand on ceremony," Marty growled. "You're holding on for your life."

As soon as he skittered across the yard, she clutched him with all her might.

"Ouch," she complained, as he sped onto the dirt trail, throwing a shower of mud and stones around their feet while he bounced across it.

"Get used to it," he cautioned her.

At first, they passed apple trees, then a forest of firs. The scent of resin freshened the air. After a mile or so, the track ended at a metalled road which bent sharply in both directions. The land was level, with nothing in sight except road, trees and sky.

Marty slowed the bike to a halt. Kat gratefully slid off it, rather inelegantly rubbing her bottom.

"That hurt," she said, adding hastily, "but it's worth it. Which way now, Marty?"

"You tell me," he said. "Who knows where Kireniat is? There are no helpful road signs. Let's flip a coin." He made a show of emptying his pockets. "Oh dear. I'm short of cash today."

"Our friends have spent it all, I bet," Kat observed. "Marty, they've probably gone to Kireniat. If we ride there, we may meet them coming back." Her eyes betrayed her fear.

"Then you'll have to hang on even tighter," Marty said. "I can outride anyone on this beast." The motorcycle was extremely well maintained and he'd enjoy a high speed ride on tarmac. "Say what you like about Russian workmanship, they know how to build a bike. We'll take the right hand road. Wherever we go, it's better than here."

As an afterthought, he told her as she remounted, "I'll be leaning over when we take a corner. Don't worry. The momentum will keep us going. Just imagine you're a sack of potatoes. Don't try leaning for me, otherwise we'll both be off."

"Okay," she said, her voice almost lost in the engine's noise as he revved the throttle.

Marty hoped she'd understood. The road zigzagged somewhat, so he took it slow at first. Thankfully, Kat did exactly as he'd asked and he sped up, arriving at a larger highway after a few miles. While straighter, this too was notable for a total absence of signage. They were still in a heavily wooded area stretching for miles ahead. The dark green trees, higher than houses, closed in on them. Marty shrugged. It was still a few hours until nightfall. They wouldn't meet a wolf yet; the creatures were nocturnal. Anyway, there was easier prey for them in these dense forests.

Again, he turned right, aiming to travel further away from the farm. The road started to slope gently downwards. Marty began to nurture hope that Kireniat lay ahead. It was logical if they were riding on the route from the mountains. After a few minutes, the trees thinned out and fields came into view, mostly pasture for horses. Darria shrubs grew freely at the roadside, some intertwined into rough hedges. In the distance, the skyscrapers of Kireniat glittered.

Marty almost punched the air, but his triumph was short-lived. The bike coughed and stuttered to a halt, almost sending him sailing over the handlebars. Kat fell forward into him.

"What happened?" she asked.

"We ran out of fuel," Marty said, winded. "There should be more in the reserve tank, enough for twenty miles. Hold on." He dismounted to look for the lever, finding it easily only to discover the machine had already drawn on its reserve. "It's empty," he told her. "Fancy hitch-hiking?" He knew it was common practice to pay for a lift, but was sure he could sweet-talk a driver into waiving the charge.

He stuck out a thumb. After ten minutes, only one car had appeared: an ancient Lada, being driven in the wrong direction. Marty fidgeted. They were sitting ducks if the kidnappers returned.

"I know what we should do," Kat said. "We can get to Kireniat in half an hour on horseback."

It was Marty's turn to feel apprehensive. "I've never ridden anything I can't put petrol into. The closest I've got to a horse is Anna's stew."

"It can't be hard. Everyone in Bazakistan can ride," Kat said, with the unshakable confidence of a girl who'd sat on a pony before she could walk. "I'm bound to find you a decent mount in that field over there. I won't let on you ate its cousin last week."

"I suspect its owners will object," Marty said.

"Do you see them anywhere?" Kat asked. "A single herdsman will look after scores of horses." She gestured in a wide arc. "He'll be back before nightfall to put them all in stables, so let's take a couple while we can. We can bring them back later."

Marty grudgingly agreed. He didn't have a better plan.

Kat made a beeline for the nearest gate. "It isn't locked," she said. "Come on, Marty. I think we're in luck."

There were just two mares in the field, a chestnut and a dappled grey. They were the short, stocky breed that was seen everywhere in Bazakistan. Kat walked over to them. She patted each one, whispering in Bazaki as if starting a conversation. Amazingly, they listened, ears flicking towards her as they spoke. The intelligent brown eyes softened.

Marty hoped they liked her. Those powerful thighs and heavy hooves would deliver a hefty kick.

"They're like most horses round here," she said. "Not much bigger than ponies. Quite old, I think. The grey is the dominant one, so if I take her, the other will follow. Marty, do you have any food in your pockets? It will help us make friends with them."

He still had a couple of apples and chunks of bread from their breakfast. "Do you want it all?" he asked.

"One apple at a time." She held the sweet fruit out to the grey mare, who munched it happily.

"See? Friends now," Kat said. She grasped the lower edge of the grey's mane and swung herself on its back in a single fluid motion. The horse stood at ease while Kat said, "Now you, Marty. Feed her first, then scramble on."

Marty approached the chestnut mare with trepidation, the remaining apple cupped in his palm. He felt her hot breath as she took it.

"Now I'm going to ride you, girl," he said. He grabbed a length of hair and attempted to vault onto her.

The poor chestnut moved half a step. Unbalanced, Marty slithered back to the ground, landing on his bottom with a thud. He was glad he was well-padded.

"This is impossible," he muttered.

Kat dismounted. "I'll hold her still," she said. She patted the chestnut before crouching down and offering Marty her shoulder for a leg up.

"Grab the mane," she said.

Marty clutched a handful of hair just as the horse swayed forward. He felt himself slipping. "I'm going to fall off," he warned Kat.

She laughed. "No you won't. Hang onto her mane. Sit up straight and relax your legs."

"Relax?" Marty spluttered.

Kat ignored the interjection. "Pat her. Tell her she's a good horse."

"Nice horse," Marty said in his best Bazaki. Patting was out of the question. He needed both hands to grip the mare's mane.

"Watch me, and do as I do," Kat said, remounting the grey. "Don't be scared. She'll know if you are."

That was easier said than done, Marty thought sourly, as his steed followed Kat's out of the gate. He heard the rattle of an engine, and broke into a cold sweat. The chestnut pricked up her ears.

"Nothing to worry about," Kat yelled. "Just a tractor going past."

Luckily, whoever was driving it thought nothing of the riders slipping through the gate. Marty took a deep breath. It failed to quell his anxiety, and he found he was still perspiring. He concentrated on staying on his mount.

To his relief, the chestnut mare appeared content to follow the grey. He had no idea how Kat communicated any sense of direction to her horse, though. She appeared to steer it by patting, stroking and whispering to it. Like all Bazakis, she rode effortlessly, seemingly born in the saddle. Horses were far more than a food source; they were beast of burden, mode of transport and leisure activity as well.

By contrast, Marty was struggling. He barely maintained his balance, grasping the horse's mane and using his thighs to grip the sides of the slippery animal. It jolted up and down. He winced in pain, glad his family was complete. He didn't rate his chances of siring children after this.

The chestnut snorted. "Nice horse," he repeated.

They stayed by the side of the road. Marty longed to reach Kireniat, which still appeared like an unattainable mirage ahead. Gradually, the city came closer. So did the black Mercedes that had appeared on the horizon.

"Kat," Marty cried out in warning.

"I know," she shouted, persuading the grey mare to stop. Dismounting with ease, she used her horse to shield herself from the sight of traffic on the highway. "Get off, Marty."

"I can't," he yelled. "Red Rum doesn't have any brakes."

The chestnut, already slowing and looking around out of curiosity, halted when Kat spoke to her. "Now," she commanded Marty.

124

He obeyed with speed, if not grace, tumbling off the animal and crouching behind it as the car sped past.

"Was Nurbolat driving?" she asked.

Marty shrugged. "How should I know? I was hiding behind Red Rum, remember?" His thighs and bottom were already stiffening, pain pulsating through them. He forced himself to ask Kat for help to remount. Cursing under his breath, he noted with envy how easily Kat climbed back onto the grey.

They were maybe five miles from the city limits, but they weren't safe yet. "Kat," he called to her. "We can't travel on the road like this. Ken has more than one car. There's a silver Merc too."

She persuaded her horse to stop. "We'll lose time if we retreat to the fields. The ground is uneven, and the hedges between them are too high to jump. The horses will have to push through them, and that takes ages."

The animals looked athletic enough to him. Whether he was bred to sit on a jumping horse was another matter. There was only one way to find out. "Humour me," he said. "We ought to try. It's safer."

Evidently, the rush hour had started. Traffic passed them every minute or so. Kat guided her mare into a wheat field, with Marty's mount following.

The ride was definitely slower now the horses were plodding through the field. Marty bounced alarmingly as his mare negotiated hidden potholes and furrows, silver-green stalks of grain appearing to part at her feet, and then entwining them. Fortunately, the first hedge was punctuated by a gate to the next field. Marty watched gratefully as Kat jumped down to open it.

"Remember the Countryside Code, bab. Make sure you close it afterwards," he said, chuckling as she gave him a filthy look.

They weren't so lucky the second time. There was no exit to the adjacent field. To Marty's dismay, Kat was proved right. The horses weren't interested in jumping. Instead, the grey began to trample her way through.

Marty was considering how he would ever stay on the chestnut once she did the same, when he heard the screech of brakes and saw a flash of silver. There was no time to warn Kat before a shot rang out. Ken Khan had found them.

Overcome by her flight instinct, the chestnut immediately leaped over the hedge she'd previously refused to jump. Caught unawares, Marty was

125

thrown off her back, landing atop the thorny hedge. The prickles drew blood as he clambered down the other side, looking around for his steed and seeing her cowering at the opposite end of the field.

By some miracle, Kat was still clinging on to the grey mare, although the horse was racing to join her companion. Marty ran after them.

"Do you have any apples left?" Kat shouted.

"Only bread," Marty replied.

"That's no good," she said. "It gives them colic. Pick some weeds – dandelions, grass, anything."

He did as he was told. The grey took the leaves he offered, but the chestnut stayed at a wary distance.

More loud bangs echoed across the field. A bullet whizzed past Marty's right ear. Another nicked the chestnut mare's leg. He saw the barrel of an AK-47 poking through the hedge they'd just navigated.

The poor chestnut squealed and recoiled in pain. Marty noticed blood trickling down a hind leg. Panicking, the mare bolted. She galloped around the edge of the field, knocking the gun sideways as she ran past. It was out of commission, but possibly not for long.

Marty saw Kat was in trouble. The grey's first instinct was to follow her friend. Kat had retained her seat on the mare, but she couldn't control the horse as it bolted. Worse, Ken was scaling the hedge, the AK-47 slung across his body. It was obvious Kat had seen the rebel leader, and equally, that there was nothing she could do to escape.

Ken cleared the hedge and steadied his Kalashnikov. Marty threw himself to the ground, waiting for the next shot. It never came. Instead, he heard two thuds in quick succession. The sound of galloping slowed.

"Marty!" It was Kat's voice.

He looked up, and across to the hedge. Kat was no longer mounted. She was standing, rubbing her head, contemplating the prone figure of Ken Khan. Bloodied, his AK-47 bent out of shape, he was lying groaning on the ground. The horses had galloped to the other side of the field.

In spite of their perilous situation, Marty chuckled. It was clear Ken had collided with Kat's horse. Ken hadn't won the argument.

"Are you all right?" he asked Kat.

"Bruised," she said. "I was thrown off."

"Join the club," Marty said. He glanced sympathetically at the injured mare. She was the innocent victim of their plight. There was no way he'd be riding her again. The two horses continued to race around the field's perimeter. They were clearly confused, spooked by the gunfire.

"We have to calm the horses," Kat said.

"No, let's run," Marty said. Ken was badly injured, had undoubtedly broken some bones, and wasn't doing anything or going anywhere fast. It was improbable that he would be on his own, though. Marty could virtually feel his own blood pressure rise. "Hurry up, bab," he said.

"We've no chance without a horse," she argued. She gathered sweet leaves for the pair, jogging alongside them, speaking soothing words.

"Kat, we have to get out of here. Ken has friends." He tugged at her arm. This was more than bravery, it was recklessness. Providence had seen Ken trampled; running too close to the mares, Kat might share his fate.

The horses slowed. Kat nodded. "The grey will be fine," she said, proving it by stopping the horse and mounting her. "Hop on behind me. You'll have to leapfrog."

Marty heard a commotion at the roadside. Ken's friends must have arrived. While the grey horse looked skittish, he had no alternative. He took a run at the tail and jumped above it, hugging Kat tight, reversing the roles they'd taken on the motorcycle. She gripped the mare's mane, urging her to trample over another hedge, towards the next field, and the next. They left Ken, his men and the highway far behind.

It was as much as Marty could do to stay on the horse. He tried to follow Kat's lead and anticipate its movements, flexing his bottom and thighs to stay connected to its warm body as it lurched up and down. Ruefully, he regretted his cavalier attitude towards Kat on the motorbike. "Where are we?" he asked Kat, a panicked edge to his voice.

"Still heading towards Kireniat," she said. "You can tell by the sun."

They arrived at a cluster of low white buildings, similar to those where they'd been held. Marty kept his sense of déjà vu to himself. He could tell this was a different farm; there were no apple trees, pigs and chickens. A woman came running out of the property, curiosity written all over her face.

"Forget her," Kat said. "Look, there's a lane from the farmhouse. It must lead somewhere."

"My guess is the highway to Kireniat," Marty said. "What are we waiting for?" He couldn't believe they'd encounter Ken's men in an entirely random section of the road.

He was right. As they neared the road, a square white patrol car came to a halt in front of them.

"No!" Kat screamed.

Chapter 29 **Kat**

"Get the horse to stop," Marty said. "The police carry arms, remember."

"All the better to kill you with," Kat said. "I'm turning back towards the farm."

"Don't be a fool," he hissed.

Two men jumped out of the car, hefting their AK-47s meaningfully. Their dark trousers, crisp white shirts and peaked caps signalled their profession. They were youngish, tall and thin, swaggering with an air of menace.

Kat knew she had no choice. They could shoot her as soon as look at her. Scowling, she dismounted from the horse and stood quietly next to it.

Marty climbed down, wincing at his bruises, then smiled and extended a hand.

He was too naive, she thought, unforgivably so. He'd visited Bazakistan often enough to know better. He was behaving as if the police were helpful individuals, the kind of public servants who would rescue his confused old mother when she wandered from her care home, and give directions to lost tourists. The innocent had nothing to fear in Marty's world. This wasn't England, however; far from it. Bazaki police were predators.

What might happen now? She and Marty were miles from the city, with no papers, no money, and a stolen horse. Without cash for bribes, she could predict what the officers would expect.

Kat regretted washing herself that morning. She kept her countenance stony, deliberately making herself unattractive. Recalling advice given on a self-defence course at school, she picked her nose. If Ulan had been dangerous without a weapon, how much more threatening were two armed killers with an entitlement complex?

If the Bazaki police didn't like you, you disappeared. Kat imagined her father's dread and disbelief when he was thrown into the cells, the agony and violence he must have suffered. Just minutes before, she'd been ecstatic at her escape from Ken Khan, looking forward to flying home to London, falling into her fiancé's arms, even seeing Erik and admitting humbly that he'd been right. Now, behind her frown, she cowered in terror.

Marty said, in perfect Russian, "Hello. I am Arystan Aliyev's business partner, and I've been kidnapped."

Chapter 30 **Marty**

Kireniat was six hours ahead of the UK. It was morning in Birmingham when Marty phoned Angela. "Hello, bab," he began, "You'll be pleased to know I've lost weight."

"Marty!" Her voice bubbled with excitement. "Where are you?"

"The British consulate in Kireniat," he told her.

"You're safe," she said. "Oh, thank goodness. When are you coming home?"

"As soon as I can get a flight," he said. It wasn't quite true. He had a visit to make first, and he'd need to return to the consulate for emergency travel documents anyway. Still, he planned to leave Kireniat the next evening at the latest. "Will you let Tim and the other children know, please?" he asked her. "I'll ring them from the hotel in an hour or so. And can you ask Tanya to call me about the flights?"

"Of course." She sounded elated. "I'll tell Erik, as well."

"I know he was right about Bazakistan, but don't take any smugness from him," Marty cautioned.

His taxi, paid for by Harry, was waiting outside to whisk Marty to his hotel. In two hours, Harry would arrive there to take him to dinner. Meanwhile, his first priority was to run a bath. He luxuriated in the hot water, ruefully examining his chafed wrists and the bruises and scratches he'd sustained on the horse ride. His hands, cut by thorns, smarted. He eased out a few splinters, then lay still, letting the bubbles dissolve his tension and aches.

For the first time in a week, he'd brushed his teeth and would change into clean clothes. Marty closed his eyes, enjoying the sensation of freedom.

The bedside phone rang. Marty leaped out of the tub, slinging the complimentary white bathrobe around his shoulders, shivering with pleasure at its velvety softness. He just managed to pick up the phone before it cut to voicemail after five rings.

"Hello, Marty, it's Ross."

"Is Kat all right?" Marty asked, the first thought that came into his head. He couldn't understand why she wouldn't be. He'd left her with the consul, after telling the man why Kat was nervous in the presence of the Bazaki police, and suggesting he ensured she didn't have to make a statement.

"Yes," Ross said, rather stiffly. "I want to thank you for helping her escape. Also, she wanted me to find out how she could get emergency travel documents without a police report. The consul's insisting the police must first record her passport as lost."

That was typical of Kat, expecting others to run errands for her. The fiancé was well under her thumb. "I've no idea," Marty said. "Sounds like red tape to me. Ask your lawyer. Why couldn't she ring me, anyway?"

"She doesn't want to speak to you," Ross said.

He was refreshingly blunt, anyway. "I suppose she's annoyed that I invoked the name of Satan himself, Harry Aliyev, to get the cops on side," Marty said. "Tell her it cut through the red tape. I'd have been in the nick and she'd have been walking five miles to Kireniat through fields if I hadn't."

"I'll let her know," Ross said. He paused. "Do forgive her, Marty. She's rather overcome with emotion right now."

"Understood," Marty said curtly. Hunger and fatigue assailed him. He replaced the handset and raided the minibar for peanuts and Scotch. Catching a glimpse of his stubble in the mirror, he hastily shaved before donning a fresh shirt and slacks. The waistband was loose. He felt smug. Angela would have to stop nagging him about diets.

He took his iPad from the desk where he'd left it a week ago, and called each of his four children on Skype. Next, he sent messages to Tanya, Erik and Amy. He added that Kat was safe and well too. Delighted emails were already hitting his inbox by the time the concierge phoned to say Mr Aliyev was waiting.

Harry wrapped him in a bear hug, his joy apparently genuine. "How are you, my friend?" he asked. "Is your hotel room as you left it?"

Marty suffered the embrace. His opinion of Harry was no higher, for all that the man's name opened doors. "The room's fine," he confirmed.

"Excellent," Harry said. "I asked them to extend the booking. You were due to return home at the weekend, weren't you?"

"I'm planning to go tomorrow," Marty said. "I don't think we have further business to discuss."

"What about the properties you wanted to see?" Harry asked.

"On hold." Marty conceded to himself that Erik was right. Darria might grow like a weed in Bazakistan, but there had to be easier places to farm it.

Harry's face betrayed disappointment. "That's a shame," he said. "I've persuaded a friend of mine to do a good deal for you. In fact, I thought we could meet him at the restaurant I've booked. It's a little French place. When Monsieur Michelin begins to give away his stars in Kireniat, this chef will be first in line, for sure."

Marty coughed to conceal a chuckle. Harry was clearly planning to take a cut for the land purchase. "I'm sorry, Harry," he said. "I'm rather tired. Couldn't we just have a steak in the hotel restaurant?" It would probably be horse. He was willing to take the risk.

"Very well," Harry agreed with barely a flicker of chagrin.

They strolled into the half-empty restaurant.

"Excuse me," Harry said, as his phone buzzed. He answered the call, occasionally interjecting in monosyllables. "Yes, thank you for letting me know," he said finally, before turning to Marty with a smile. "Great news, my friend."

"What's that?" Marty was intrigued.

"The army have raided the place where they held you. All the extremists are dead."

Marty was about to say they weren't extremists, then thought better of it. Local politics was none of his business. His sympathies hardly lay with Ken Khan, anyway. It was impossible to believe he and Kat would have left the farm alive if they hadn't taken matters into their own hands. "That's good to hear," he said. "Although, Harry, there is one other thing I'd like to know."

"What would that be?" Harry asked, unashamedly curious.

"Are the horses all right? The chestnut especially, as she sustained a wound."

"My friend, I'm glad you asked," Harry said with discernible warmth. He evidently loved horses as much as any of his countrymen. "I am told it was just a scratch. Both the chestnut and grey have been returned to their owners. I'll make sure they're appropriately compensated."

"Let me know if I owe you anything," Marty said.

"I won't hear of it," Harry replied. "You were our guest in Bazakistan, and if I may say so," he lowered his voice, "at the highest level, there is a great deal of embarrassment at your difficulties here. So let's celebrate your release." He called the sommelier to select some red wine. "A decent vintage, please."

The ruby liquid was poured into glasses. Harry raised one. "To liberty!" he said.

"To liberty," Marty echoed, marvelling at Harry's hypocrisy. He could barely wait for the morning, to receive his documents and take a cab to the airport. There was another task to perform first, but he had no intention of telling Harry about that.

Chapter 31 **Marty**

In Marty's opinion, the best feature of the sixties bungalow was that it was mostly screened from view. Tall birch trees around the substantial garden gave privacy from the highway nearby, the adjacent vodka factory, and the fields that bordered one side of the square plot. His taxi swung into a sweeping gravel drive and halted by the front door.

"Wait here," Marty said, giving the driver a fistful of notes. "There will be more later," he promised.

Although the weather was dry and mild, Marty had zipped up his Barbour parka and pulled the hood over his balding head, all the better to hide it from prying eyes. Harry would imagine he was on his way to the airport. To make sure Harry was at the factory rather than at home with his loving wife, Marty had just phoned him on his landline and exchanged pleasantries.

The doorbell played the opening notes of The Rite of Spring by Stravinsky. Marty congratulated himself on remembering it from his schooldays. Great things had been expected from him at grammar school, until he'd chosen to leave at sixteen to set up in business. Despite his recent tribulations, he was happy he'd made the right choice.

Through the swirly glass of the door, Marty saw a blonde figure. He readied his foot to push the door ajar as soon as it opened the tiniest sliver.

A chain rattled, momentarily causing him to shudder at memories of his cell. A bolt was drawn back. The lady of the house stood before him, long flaxen hair limp around her fine-boned face. Her jade-green dress matched the eyes that stared at him, alarmed.

"Hello, Maria," he said.

She was silent, her mouth dropping in shock.

Marty no longer had any doubts, and nor, it seemed, did she. "I'm not a ghost," he said, "although you'd rather I were, wouldn't you? May I come in?"

He used his knee to widen the door's aperture, walking inside. "Actually, that wasn't a question," he said.

She recovered her composure and looked at him with distaste. "What do you want?" she asked.

"Just a cup of tea and a chat." Seeing her recoil from him, he added, "That really is all. I have things to tell you, and others I want to ask. Indulge my curiosity, Maria."

"Come in, then," she said, acceding to the inevitable. He was already standing in the lobby, after all. "Just don't call me Maria. I don't want to remember." Her eyes were fierce, like a panicked animal's.

"Very well. Marina." She'd moved on from Sasha quickly enough, then, but Marty resisted a jibe. He needed answers, not a fight.

"You'd better sit in the drawing room," Marina said. "You know where it is." Her lips, painted a soft pink shade, twitched at the corners.

She looked nothing like her age. How much was artifice, pots and potions of the sort his wife enjoyed using, he had no idea. A casual observer would think she'd had an easy life, but it was clear Marina felt the old times had been much easier than today.

"I'll come with you into the kitchen if you don't mind," Marty said. "I like to make my own tea. I'm quite particular about it." He would prefer to forgo a seasoning of crushed paracetamol tablets, for instance.

Marina gave no indication she'd considered any such thing. She led him into the kitchen, a large room overlooking the blind concrete walls of the factory. Once, he recalled, she'd been proud of its fitted pine furniture. Sasha had made it for her. That was gone, replaced with glossy black units, granite worktops and steel appliances. Angela occasionally showed him photographs of such fixtures in magazines; he assumed the look was trendy the world over. What was plain, and presumably essential to Marina and Harry, was its costliness. The huge range cooker and American-style fridge were exclusive European brands.

Instead of a kettle or samovar, there was a chrome tap that produced boiling water at the press of a button. Marina filled two red china mugs and dunked teabags in them. This was unlike the serious ceremony with leaves that she had favoured in the past, and which was still observed by Erik to this day.

She tipped milk and sugar into his mug without asking him if he wanted any. Marty watched carefully to make sure that was all she used.

The drawing room had changed too. Once white and utilitarian, decorated with her children's scribbled artwork, it was now painted red. There were gold and turquoise velvet sofas, a huge patterned Bazaki carpet. The only pictures were framed still lives and portraits, mostly done in oils. A couple of photographs showed attractive young people. Who were they?

Marina noticed his gaze shifting to them. "Arystan's children," she murmured.

Marty laughed harshly. "That's not all of them, is it? Anyway, where are yours?"

She dropped her eyes. "Arystan doesn't want them mentioned." Her mouth twitched again. "Tell me, Marty, do you have news of them? How are they?"

Marty was tempted to say they were both heroin addicts in prison. He decided to tell the truth. "They're both fine young people. Erik is a scientist and Kat is engaged to a rich man. She resembles you in many ways."

"I'm so glad," Marina said. Her frown lifted. "I worried about them so much. I looked online, on Facebook and Google, but there wasn't a trace of them."

"You were looking for Belovs, weren't you? Small wonder you couldn't find them. They took English names," Marty said.

"What are they?"

Marty ignored the question. He added brutally, "Their success is no thanks to you. You abandoned both of them. They were heartbroken, believing you dead."

"What choice did I have?" she asked. "My husband, the love of my life, died at the hands of a firing squad. I was left destitute. When Arystan offered marriage, it was the only way out."

"You could have turned to me," Marty said. "I'd been paying your lawyers for two years, remember?" The fees, and 'commissions', had cost him a small fortune.

"Really?" she asked, her voice icy with cynicism. "You're hardly showing me mercy now. You wouldn't have done then, either. Nothing you did was for Sasha, or for me. You got exactly what you wanted. You're still distributing Snow Mountain for Arystan. I tell you, it won't be for long. Distributors are two a penny. I'll persuade him to find another." She practically spat out her threat.

"He won't," Marty said. He doubted she held sway over Harry these days. His business partner was clearly bored with her and playing away. He came to the point. "I own the Snow Mountain brand. I had my solicitor register the trademark in practically every country in the world

136

outside of Bazakistan." He owed Katherine Evans a crate of champagne, or maybe vodka. "Ask your lawyer to confirm it, if you want. Harry needs me more than I need him."

He paused to make sure she'd digested the implications. "I've got news for you, Marina. I think you wanted me dead. I'm not sure why. Perhaps you thought I'd recognise you and tell your children their mother had risen from the grave. They might have asked awkward questions."

She didn't deny it.

He continued, "I've written a letter, and sent two copies by courier this morning, one to my wife and one to my lawyer in Birmingham. You can't intercept it, because the freight plane's left Kireniat already. I've emailed it to my secretary too, protected with a password that I texted to her. All of those individuals are under strict instructions only to open that letter on my death. In addition, if the circumstances of my demise are in the least bit suspicious, they're to issue the contents of the letter as a press release. The Daily Mail could make a very juicy headline of it. So," he smiled, "I expect you'd like to know what the letter says."

Marina shrugged. "Not really."

"You should be more inquisitive," Marty said. "I've written everything I know about you."

Marina remained cool. "Some fanciful conjecture, I'm sure."

"I may have made guesses to fill in a few gaps. There's enough to make you very supportive of my well-being. For instance. You say Sasha was the love of your life, but you got over him quickly enough. You didn't just leap into Harry's bed. You've been having an affair with Ken Khan, the terrorist."

"You've no proof," she said, her face impassive.

"I bet I could find it if I tried. You forget he was holding me at that orchard outside Kireniat."

Her face registered shock. The information must be new to her, then. "There's more to that story than you know," he said. "I'll tell you later. Anyway, if we're talking about proof, it won't be up to me to get it. More critically from your point of view, at the first suggestion that you were involved with Ken Khan, the police and secret service will be looking for evidence. When they ask questions, it isn't over a nice cup of tea. They won't be impressed. Nor will Harry. Being the control freak he is, he'll kick you out, if he doesn't kill you first." Harry would probably welcome an excuse to be free from the confines of his marriage. He'd wanted her when she was unattainable. Having won his prize, he'd lost interest.

"You don't understand," Marina wailed, tears welling. "Can you imagine what it's been like for me, submitting to Arystan's touch when he makes my skin crawl? It's obvious he has blood on his hands from Sasha's death."

"You chose to marry him," Marty pointed out. He felt awkward, uncomfortable in the presence of a grown woman crying. Nevertheless, his sympathy was wafer-thin.

"In any case," Marina begged, "please say nothing to Erik and Katya. I can't bear them to know."

"Make it worth my while," Marty said. "I want to carry on my business unhindered."

Her secrets weren't burdensome to him. Sharing them with her children wasn't necessarily in their best interests. While they'd loved their mother, did they really need to know what she'd done? They'd grieved for her already. "Incidentally," he said, "I wasn't Ken's only prisoner."

"Yes," she said slowly, showing no concern. "There was a British girl too, wasn't there?"

"Katya has a British passport now," he replied.

The blood drained from her face.

Chapter 32 **Kat**

Arman Khan gave Kat a lift to the airport. Reassuringly, he drove a Jeep rather than a Mercedes. He liked to drive through deserts, he told her, and go cross-country skiing in the snowy mountains.

Arman had been most solicitous all morning, taking her to the consulate and pulling strings to find her a seat on the next Bazakair flight. She shouldn't worry about the commercial court hearing last Friday, Arman had said; he'd turned up and arranged a postponement. Kat suspected Ted Edwards had had strong words with him. This was borne out when Arman told her she must not imagine he was related to Ken Khan. Their surname was common because many ethnic Bazakis claimed descent from Genghis.

They drove past Kireniat University, seeing perhaps a thousand students outside it with pro-democracy placards. One of them threw a missile at the Jeep. Arman swerved, managing to avoid it. Flames flared into the air where it had landed.

Kat's heart stopped. She wanted to scream, but all that emerged was a fearful whimper.

"Don't worry, I'll step on the gas," Arman said, doing just that. The Jeep jolted forward, causing demonstrators to jump out of its path. "You know, that Molotov cocktail came our way by mistake. The students think we're with the authorities. They're angry at Ken Khan's death."

"What do you think?" Kat asked, a tremor creeping into her voice. Thankfully, Arman had driven past the students, and was speeding down the broad highway to the airport. Her feelings about the revolution were mixed: delight that it might still happen, tempered with relief that no other hostages would suffer at Ken Khan's hands. Captivity had hardly been a holiday camp. It was difficult not to take it personally.

If Arman shared her support for the rebels, he wasn't going to admit it. "This government provides stability," he replied. "When you see what's happened to other nations in the region, you learn to appreciate it."

The business community evidently didn't share his confidence. Bazakair flights, she had learned, were fully booked today. Tourists, businessmen and expatriates alike were rushing to fly home. Luckily, Arman's aunt was married to one of the airline's directors. At his insistence, a seat became available.

The last time she'd departed from Kireniat airport, it had been a collection of huts clustered around a dusty runway. Now, there was an airy new terminal designed by a celebrated British architect. Arman made sure a Bazakair employee escorted Kat to the club lounge, a spacious room overlooking the flight strip. The lounge was mercifully free of the armed police guarding the departures area. It was busy, however, full of suited men speaking too loudly on their phones and drinking too much free whisky. To her relief, Marty wasn't one of them. Kat ordered complimentary champagne and watched the CNN news channel on a large, wall-mounted screen.

"An Army raid on the kidnappers' hideout resulted in six deaths," the announcer intoned. "Bazaki authorities say they've foiled a Muslim extremist plot led by Ken Khan, a terror suspect believed by the government to have trained under the Taliban. Now, we ask British businessman Martyn Bridges how he feels."

Marty was standing outside the British consulate in Kireniat. "I'm just glad to be free, and I want to go home to Birmingham," he said. "My wife's planning a party."

The screen cut away to a scene in Birmingham, a gracious, white-painted detached mansion decorated with balloons and banners. "Welcome home, Marty," the largest said.

Ross hadn't suggested any kind of celebration. They'd said little to each other since her release, and in fact, he'd been extremely defensive when she'd challenged him about his intention to pay her ransom. Kat walked away from the TV and over to the window, downing her drink quickly and helping herself to another on the way. The floor to ceiling plate glass was so clean, she barely noticed it was there. Beyond the airfield, downtown Kireniat shimmered in the sun. There was still snow on the distant mountains behind it. She sipped her champagne, wishing the bubbles would lift her spirits, as she gazed at the country of her birth. She'd never come back, no matter what awaited her in London.

Chapter 33 **Marty**

Marty's flight was the last of the day, with a Middle Eastern airline that stopped in Dubai. On another occasion, he might have left the plane there to do business. This time, he was keen to return to Angela. He asked an air hostess for advice on choosing gifts for his wife. Buying for a woman was a minefield, requiring specialist help. Between them, they selected Angela's favourite perfume and a pricy cosmetic set.

There was no question of infidelity from Angela. He'd known her long enough to trust her completely. She had been his secretary for decades, carrying a torch for him and hooking him swiftly once his first wife died. Marty had just gone with the flow. After all, he needed a warm bed, a tidy house and tea on the table when he returned from work. While he wasn't in love, she was good company and made the most of herself. Marriage hadn't dimmed her eagerness to please.

Marina, on the other hand, was beautiful, heart-stoppingly so even now. She was accustomed to using men for her own ends. He'd believed Kat was heading the same way. Now, he wasn't so sure. She really seemed devoted to Snow Mountain vodka. Perhaps she could work for him after all. Should he use his leverage over Marina to encourage Harry to hand over the factory to Kat? Marty shook his head. It was fraught with difficulty. Harry would never do it, and anyway, the engineer was an efficient factory manager. Far better to keep the threat of exposure hanging over Marina. She'd wanted him dead – let her sweat.

The airline did not serve alcohol, but they turned a blind eye to passengers who brought their own. This had been explained at the check-in desk. Marty drank the perfectly acceptable red wine he'd bought in the duty-free shop at Kireniat, and took a sleeping tablet as the plane left Dubai. He slipped easily into deep sleep.

Chapter 34 **Davey**

Davey unlocked the black door, determined that this was the last time he'd stay at the pied-à-terre in Mayfair. The smell of paint was even more pervasive than before, assailing him before he ascended the stairs to the first floor flat. He threw open the French doors, about to step onto the balcony. Just in time, he realised that, while its railings were intact, the balcony floor was missing. He remembered Dee saying the wooden planks were rotten.

Alana arrived a few minutes later. She was wearing her running kit, carrying working clothes, killer heels and bag in a backpack. Davey buzzed her into the flat without a greeting. He hadn't really wanted to see her that evening. In fact, he didn't want to see her at all, except in a professional capacity, and he was going to tell her.

"Hey, I love jogging beside the Thames on these sunny evenings," Alana said. "I can't get over all the losers sitting in traffic jams on the Victoria Embankment." She smirked, clearly in a good mood. "Let's have a bourbon – a snifter, I believe you Brits call it." She raided the dining room for the whiskey and glasses, apparently oblivious to Davey's subdued demeanour.

Davey glowered at her. He grabbed his glass and knocked back the drink.

"This is a building site," Alana complained. "There are paint pots everywhere, and the smell makes me sick. Let's go to my place." She took a sip. "You know I've got a great sound system. We'll play Metallica. Not my preference, maybe, but I'll live with it to see your mojo rising."

It was like the buzz of a particularly annoying insect. She no longer held any glamour for him. He gulped down a second glass. "No, Alana," he said. "It's over. You've got what you wanted from Saxton Brown. You're not keeping me dangling on a string any longer." He rose to his feet. "Finish your drink, then leave."

Alana had the temerity to laugh. "I call the shots, baby. What's Laura going to say when I…"

Davey interrupted her. "I'll sort that out. Lie if I have to."

"It won't work," she said triumphantly. "I've recorded every word of this conversation on my phone."

Davey's eyes hardened. "You bitch," he spat. "Give it to me." Was she bluffing? Although he hadn't seen her use the phone, he wasn't prepared to take a chance. He reached for her backpack. It had to be in there.

Inside the backpack, he found her handbag, the phone neatly strapped into a pocket. Alana grappled with him as his fingers curled around it.

Davey shoved her away. An empty paint pot caught her off balance. She tripped, flying out of the French door, plunging two floors to the flagstones outside the basement flat below.

There was a crunching sound. For a split second, Davey stared in disbelief at Alana's prone figure. She wasn't moving. He reached for the bourbon, swiftly filling and draining his glass a third time, before dialing 999. Without stopping to think, he finished the bottle.

He was kneeling by Alana's side when the first paramedic, a young woman called Sarah, arrived on a bicycle.

"An ambulance is on its way," Sarah assured him. She shone a torch in Alana's eyes. "Alana, can you hear me?"

Above them, pedestrians strolled past, seemingly oblivious to the quiet drama below. Noting the blood seeping onto the creamy flagstones, Sarah informed Davey that Alana's skull was probably fractured. The good news, perhaps, was that she was still breathing and very much alive.

Within minutes, both an ambulance and an uninvited police car had arrived.

"I'm the CEO of Saxton Brown and Alana Green is my opposite number at Bishopstoke. They're both insurance companies," Davey explained to the two police constables. "We were having a drink and a chat about a deal we're doing. Alana unfortunately overbalanced."

It was almost true, but omitted a great deal too. As Davey anticipated, however, his position in the City ensured he was believed. He was given a lift to West End Central, the local police station situated among the tailors of Savile Row, to make a witness statement.

He had a pounding headache by the time he was seated in the interview room with the police constable who was to take his statement on video.

"Ready?" the man asked, his expression eager. He was young, in his early twenties at most.

"I feel rather unwell, actually," Davey admitted. To his alarm, the words sounded slurred.

"How much did you drink?" the constable asked.

"Three glasses of bourbon," Davey replied. It was as much as he could recall. "I'm not drunk." Downing whiskey on an empty stomach had evidently done him no favours, though.

"Perhaps not, but I suggest you make your statement at another time," the officer said. "I can book an appointment for you tomorrow?"

He was about to agree when there was a knock on the door. The second constable reappeared. "We have a witness who heard an argument," he said. "You do not have to say anything. But, it may harm your defence if…"

As the caution was given, a wave of nausea overcame Davey, pinning him to his seat.

Chapter 35 **Marty**

As a child, Marty had helped his mother clean a house on Wellington Road. The properties were huge, square and white; they reminded him of iced cakes. He'd been fascinated by the endless series of rooms within, connected to different floors by dumbwaiters and accessed through doors that appeared to lead to cupboards. There were toilets inside as well as out. How could a family need more than one bathroom? When his mother found no more polishing for him to do, he'd been sent to play in the garden, a wide expanse of lawn bounded by rhododendrons. To a five-year-old, the space had seemed as large as a park. "These houses at the top of the hill are the best in Birmingham," his mother had said. "Imagine the parties they have here!"

He'd dreamed of jam sandwiches, jelly and trifle, hide and seek among the shrubs, but the invitation never came. Snow Mountain had enabled him to buy on Wellington Road for his growing family, however. Now, he and Angela rattled around in their six bedroom, four bathroom property. They could easily accommodate a hundred guests at a party. Looking around his garden, Marty guessed there were even more.

By the summerhouse, a covers band was playing Duran Duran numbers. The music boomed out over a happy throng, laughing and chatting in the sunshine.

"Like it?" Angela asked.

He nodded, a wave of affection sweeping over him. He had a soft spot for eighties pop, the New Romantics in particular. She'd not only remembered that, she'd ensured there were bottles of craft ale at the travelling bar she'd booked. While a couple of mixologists prepared cocktails for his younger guests, Marty and his drinking buddies indulged in Two Towers Mild.

Angela looked radiant. As ever, she was immaculately turned out, her short hair curled and golden, her make-up carefully applied to give the illusion of sparkling-eyed youth. She was wearing an outfit Marty especially liked, a black leather jacket and shimmering dress the colour of rain clouds. He appreciated the trouble she'd taken.

Tim, his eldest, wandered over. "Glad you're drinking the good stuff," Marty said, noting the bottle in his hand.

"First and last for me," Tim said. "I'm driving." He turned to Angela. "Why aren't you two dancing?"

Marty sniggered as Angela said, "Chance would be a fine thing."

Tim rolled his eyes. "Guess you can't teach an old dog new tricks. Let's do the honours then, Angela, you and me. First on the dance floor."

"Well, the lawn, anyway," she said, linking her arm in his. They swayed to the music, Tim's tousled curls bobbing alongside Angela's. He'd sported locks like that at Tim's age, Marty recalled; a mullet, in fact. Dolefully, he touched his bald pate.

Lost hair and jet lag couldn't stop him grinning, though. At last, Angela seemed to be accepted as one of the family.

It was a warm evening, the scent of roses signalling that spring would turn to summer soon. Erik and Amy were lounging on a swinging seat by the rose bushes, apparently deep in conversation. Marty noticed his business partner pick a single red flower for the marketing manager. Amy's reaction went unseen as friends and neighbours accosted Marty, shaking his hand and hugging him, bringing him more drinks. When he next spied them, the pair were joining the dancers, evidently cajoled by Angela.

"Are those two an item?" Angela asked, appearing by his side.

Marty shrugged. "God knows. Why don't you ask them?"

He'd greeted Erik when the young man arrived but it was hours before they had a chance to exchange another word. By then, most of the guests had gone. Marty's youngest daughter, Milly, was helping Amy and Angela tidy the inevitable debris from the celebrations. Marty had opened another beer and settled on the swing seat.

"I'm sorry my sister wasn't here," Erik said.

"No need to apologise," Marty drawled. Somehow, he'd suspected Kat wouldn't show up.

"I'm glad you were there for her," Erik said. He sighed. "I did tell you there was turmoil in Bazakistan, but you wouldn't listen."

"You were right," Marty admitted. "Still, the army took out Ken Khan."

"So they say," Erik replied. "I wouldn't be too sure."

Marty grimaced. "It really is the place for darria. The stuff still grows like a weed."

Erik looked worried.

"No need to panic," Marty said. "I won't be farming it there any time soon. I'm not convinced the old man can maintain his grip much longer." Even if he did, the President couldn't outsmart the Grim Reaper forever.

146

What would happen when he died? "I want to look for alternative supplies. It can't be too difficult."

"You're thinking a little research will help us find a place with similar geology and climate?" Erik asked.

"Exactly. Or the aspects that are crucial to successful darria cultivation, anyway. Maybe it will take a little longer to source enough for a product launch, or we'll launch it in phases. Let's meet for a beer tomorrow and we can discuss our options." Dusk was falling and Marty's eyelids were beginning to droop.

"Actually, I think we'll have to change those launch plans," Erik said. "Amy agrees. We were going to run PR trips to Bazakistan, remember? She won't do it now."

It was a blow. Marty frowned. He'd forgotten the press junkets they'd planned. There was no way he was leading lifestyle journalists into the den of Bazakistan's revolutionaries, even if they could be persuaded to risk it. "I'm not going back any time soon," he said. "Let's see what other ideas Amy has. What do you think?" As part of his succession planning, he needed Erik to take more responsibility. He didn't want to work forever. Perhaps he should ask his children to be involved in the darria joint venture, too. It would give him a chance to move Amy to another part of his empire, if that was still what she wanted.

Angela appeared with a couple of carrier bags. "Will you take some food home, Erik? I've packed a few things for Amy as well."

"She could use a little more flesh on her bones, couldn't she?" Marty said.

"Unlike you," Angela said. "It's a six hundred calorie day tomorrow."

"But I've lost weight," Marty protested.

"Not enough," she rebuked him.

"And I thought I would take you out to lunch," he teased. "I'll have to find a place that serves bread and water. Actually, I've just come back from one of those."

Angela laughed, but was unmoved. "Take me out the day after," she said.

Marty grinned. "You see what married life is like?" he said to Erik. "It hasn't taken long to settle back into it."

"Oh, it doesn't seem so bad," Erik said. "Thanks for the party, Angela. I'd better be walking Amy home." Their colleague had appeared, almost groaning under the weight of the provisions Angela had pressed on her.

"I'll give you a lift," Marty said.

Angela stared at the bottle in his hand. "You will not. I'll call a taxi. And congratulations on the baby, Amy."

"What have I missed?" Marty asked.

Chapter 36 **Davey**

Davey had weekly lunches at a City club with two of his largest investors. Anwen represented a major private equity group, and Sajid handled the portfolio of a sovereign wealth fund. While they made an unlikely pair – she a short, buxom Welsh woman and he a tall, lithe greybeard of Pakistani origin – they had an informal business partnership. They often collaborated on their investments, and tended to hold sway over Saxton Brown's other shareholders. Davey would have preferred a meal at the Duck & Waffle, but acceded to their strong preference for the more secure environment offered by Anwen's club.

She had emailed ahead to say she'd arranged a private dining room this week. Davey arrived to find it was a glass-walled meeting room laid out for a meal. He guessed an important announcement was on the cards.

Anwen and Sajid were already seated at the table, conferring. They rose to their feet to shake his hand, then promptly sat down again. He was mildly surprised that Anwen's usual air-kiss wasn't forthcoming.

"Sparkling water?" she asked, knowing his preference and pouring it before he replied. Her straight dark hair swished in front of her face. Davey was reminded of Alana's bob. He shivered.

According to gossip, directors' lunches had been long and alcoholic affairs when he began working at Veritable Insurance two decades before. As a keen young graduate, Davey had never had the opportunity to find out. Now he'd risen to the dizzy heights of the boardroom, lunches were speedier affairs typified by their sobriety. Davey's investors wouldn't waste time on idle chit-chat when they could be doing deals to deliver profits to their masters.

A teenage waitress took their order: a starter and main course each. It was unlikely that anyone would hang around for pudding after the meal, although espressos might be drunk.

Once the trio were alone again, Anwen cut to the chase. "I imagine there's been talk in the insurance world about Alana's Green's recent accident," she said. "It's certainly the subject of gossip within the investment community."

"I understand you were there," Sajid said. "Would you care to tell us more?"

Davey nodded. It was crucial to keep his investors on side. They could hear the whole story, except for the affair and the argument that had sent

Alana plunging over the edge. "I'm selling part of the business to Alana, as you know," he began. "We decided to have a drink together."

"At your sister's flat?" Anwen asked, eyes wide.

"Yes, I've been supervising the decorators," Davey lied. "We drank bourbon, rather too much, as it happened. Alana wanted fresh air. She stepped onto the balcony. I'd forgotten the builders were removing the rotten base. When she fell, I tried to stop her." He shook his head. "It was no good."

Davey recalled the interview in the police station taking a darker turn. He'd denied an argument, of course. He must have raised his voice to stop her, he'd said. As for the affair, he hadn't mentioned it. He hoped Alana wouldn't either, although he feared the day when she was well enough to be interviewed. There was no guessing what she'd say. It would be her word against his, but it might sway the police investigation. The impact on his marriage would be even worse. He hid his anxiety behind a smile.

A plate of oysters was brought, the shellfish tidily presented on a bed of crushed ice decorated with seaweed and lemon quarters. The investors were to share it. Davey had smoked salmon. Again, the conversation ground to a halt until the waitress left.

"Would it be true to say," Anwen asked, "that the police are still making enquiries at this stage?"

"Yes," Davey admitted. He took care to keep his tone and expression neutral. "There's no suggestion I've done anything wrong."

"Other than, possibly, getting a little too close to Alana Green? Rumours are rife in the City," Anwen said. She eased an oyster from its shell with a tiny fork.

"We have to safeguard our assets. We can't afford to let you do sweetheart deals with your friends," Sajid said. "The sale to Bishopstoke Insurance is on hold as of now. We are suspending you on full pay while we investigate."

"We're also considering our options for Saxton Brown," Anwen said.

"Yes," Sajid added. "I'm minded to put it up for sale. We may combine it with our other insurance investments to do so – we have interests in Bermuda too. We'll achieve a good price by selling the whole business as a going concern and throwing it open to bidders."

"A very good price," Anwen echoed. "Better than we might expect from Bishopstoke, unless they up the ante, naturally. Oh, look." A tiny pearl lurked behind her oyster in its shell. "Isn't that lucky?"

"I don't believe in luck," Sajid said, his eyes cold.

"Meanwhile," Anwen said, ignoring the comment, "we're not parachuting in a new CEO to cover for you. We hope the suspension will be brief. Therefore, we are trusting Ross Pritchard and Charles Satterthwaite to run the business. I will call them personally each day at 7.30am for an update."

Davey suspected Ross and Charles would be as impressed as he was. He wondered how he'd break the news to Laura.

Chapter 37 **Kat**

"Bermuda?" Kat asked, raising an eyebrow.

"I'm sorry, darling," Ross said. "Anwen told me this morning. I'm booked on the 3pm flight. There's just time to pack a suitcase."

Disbelieving, she clutched his arm as he opened the wardrobe. "Who's Anwen?"

"She represents our biggest investors," Ross said. "Basically, she tells the others what to do. Right now, she's asked Charles and me to run the company, because Davey Saxton's on the way out. He had an affair with Alana Green, they had a fight, and she fell off his balcony."

"No way," Kat said. She looked askance at Ross. If stuffy bald Davey Saxton could cheat on his wife, how did she know her handsome fiancé hadn't succumbed to temptation?

"The boys in blue are involved, needless to say," Ross said. "They think Davey pushed her."

"Did he?" Kat asked.

"Probably," Ross said. "Alana had it coming. She's so aggressive, all my friends left Veritable Insurance after her company bought it. Charles' only comment was to ask why anyone would wait so long to throw her off a balcony. That was after he'd got over the shock of a seven thirty wake-up call from Anwen every morning." He shrugged. "It makes no difference to me. I'm up early for the gym anyway. And I'm in with a shout for Davey Saxton's job." He smirked. "Charles is just a geek. They can't give it to him. So if Anwen says jump, I'm doing it."

"But you're away in Dublin this weekend on your friend's stag do, and I've only just got home from Bazakistan," Kat said.

"Exactly," Ross said. "I would have taken you to Bermuda, but I thought you'd prefer to be in London after all that travelling. I'll just fly straight to Dublin after the business trip. You can have a few days' peace and quiet."

She'd have a few days enjoying herself with his credit card, Kat thought mulishly, followed by evenings sampling vodka cocktails in the interest of research. Snow Mountain might be out of reach, but she was surer than ever that her future lay in the distilling trade. Perhaps she should visit Erik in Birmingham. She owed him an apology. Although he

152

was too kind to remind her, he'd been right about Bazakistan all along. Was he right about other matters too? When she'd phoned him from the consulate in Kireniat, he'd told her in no uncertain terms that she was marrying the wrong man.

Her dilemma was resolved with a call from Amy.

"It's really sweet of you to ring," Kat said. They'd drifted apart since their flat-sharing days. Kat knew she hadn't always been a good friend to Amy. She also felt Amy was overly familiar with Ross, but that no longer seemed important.

"Erik suggested it," Amy said. "I'm coming into London this weekend, and I need somewhere to stay."

"I have a spare room," Kat offered. "Two spare rooms, actually." Ross' apartment was substantial. "Take your pick."

They met at Euston station that Friday evening. "I thought we could have cocktails on Charlotte Street," Kat said, "then walk back to the flat. We can do some damage to Ross' wine collection." She added, "He knows a lot about wine."

"As a suave man about town would, to impress the ladies," Amy said, seemingly unimpressed. Whatever Ross may have been to her in the past, she evidently didn't care much for him now. "As long as it's white and dry, I'll drink it."

Just south of the BT Tower, Fitzrovia's streets were mostly quiet and residential, but there were a few roads lined with media companies and buzzing bars. Friday night queues were already beginning. Without a booking, they were lucky to find seats in a new Mexican café around the corner from the flat.

"I can't believe the prices," Amy admitted, after they'd ordered enchiladas and a pitcher of margaritas. "They're double what I'd pay in Birmingham."

"We'll stick it on my credit card. Ross pays it off every month," Kat said. Her engagement ring sparkled in the candlelight, another reminder of her fiancé's wealth and her dependence on him. "So, tell me all about the baby," she commanded. "Isn't it exciting?"

"I can't wait to see him," Amy said. "It was a shock when Dad told me, though. Even now, it doesn't feel real. Most people have months to look forward to the arrival of a sibling. When I meet George tomorrow, I'll have had a week."

"You said it was a surprise to your father too," Kat pointed out.

"Yes, he'd split up with Dee, and she didn't tell him until she went into labour." Amy gulped her margarita. "I guess she was cross with him. It's ironic that he left her because he didn't want to be tied down, but now he's pining for her and she won't take him back."

"That's too bad," Kat said. "I thought you wanted him to get together with your mum again."

"There's no chance of that," Amy said. "They've both moved on."

Kat squeezed her hand. "At least you've still got both your parents."

Amy returned the squeeze and topped up Kat's glass. "Have another drink."

The margaritas led inevitably to champagne back at the flat. Ross had indulged in a dual temperature wine fridge, stashing twelve bottles of Dom Pérignon in the cooler section.

Amy looked appreciative. "That's eye-wateringly expensive. Ross won't mind, will he?" she asked.

"He can afford it," Kat said, pulling the cork and lavishly filling two flutes with bubbles. "Bottoms up!" They were soon giggling like schoolgirls.

"This is just like the old days," Amy said.

"It was Prosecco then," Kat said. "And vodka." She sighed. "We never really spoke about Snow Mountain, did we? Has Erik said anything about it?"

"Only that he wished you'd forget it," Amy said. "He was really upset when he found out you'd gone back to Bazakistan, especially without Ross."

Kat poured herself more champagne. She knew Erik was right. "It was my dream to get the vodka distillery back," she said. "I used to hang around there all the time as a child. The engineers explained how the plant worked. My father's secretary showed me letters from foreign celebrities saying how much they enjoyed drinking Snow Mountain. I truly believed it was my destiny to make vodka and travel the world as an ambassador for the product." She sniffed. Champagne usually lifted her mood, but not now. Tears were threatening. "Erik's right, of course. Kireniat isn't safe. My parents died. I was kidnapped. I can't get ownership of Snow Mountain, and I'm lucky to be alive. I have to let my dream go."

"Could you make vodka here, in London?" Amy asked.

"That's exactly what I'm thinking. You can distil it anywhere with the right equipment," Kat mused. "Marty said he could make it in Birmingham. I presumed he was joking."

"Marty's sharp," Amy said. "I enjoy working for him, actually. He's a good boss, not like the slave driver I had at Veritable Insurance." She grimaced. "You seemed to detest him before, but he helped you escape from those terrorists in Bazakistan, didn't he? Do you still hate him?"

"I don't know," Kat admitted. "I'd have gone insane in that cell without him. His sense of humour was all that made it bearable. And then…"

Remembering Ulan, she shivered. Marty hadn't hesitated to fight him, despite being drugged. He'd been there when she needed him, but not for her parents. She shook her head, frowning. "I had to trust him then, but I can't forget what he did in the past. He let my parents die simply to save his business. Erik's naïve to put any faith in him."

"Erik and Marty have different priorities," Amy said. "Neither of them is perfect. Erik's a talented scientist, but he's also a saint, and that's no way to earn living."

Kat rolled her eyes. "He was always altruistic."

"Precisely," Amy said, "And Marty's very focused on money, but they've figured out how to work together. You know, Marty's basically kind-hearted. I can't believe he wouldn't have tried to save your parents."

Kat pursed her lips. "Can we talk about something else?" she asked. Maybe she'd been wrong about Marty. She was beginning to think it wasn't her only mistake. "Let's open another bottle," she suggested.

The second bottle slipped down as easily as the first. Ross would never miss it. There were another ten just like it in the fridge.

The predictable consequence was a hangover on Saturday morning. Kat staggered out of bed at ten, only thinking to shake Amy awake once she'd dosed herself with Nurofen and black coffee from Ross' state of the art espresso machine. "What time are you seeing your father?" she asked.

"OMG," Amy said. "In five minutes." She named the coffee shop where they'd arranged to meet. Fortunately, it was on Charlotte Street.

"Look, I'll pop down there to meet and greet him," Kat said breezily. "Grab some ibuprofen, and join us when you're ready to face the world."

"That'll be next week," Amy complained.

Kat relented. "I'll make you a coffee first. And stick some lippie on. I always say, if you look good, you feel good."

155

The meeting place was modish, its walls bare brick, the décor faux-industrial. Kat easily recognised Charles. They'd enjoyed a cigarette together outside the Savoy at Saxton Brown's Christmas party, a select but rather grand affair.

"Amy's on her way," she said, before he had a chance to ask. "Congratulations about the baby."

"Thank you," he said. "Can I get you anything?" He gestured to the counter, where beans from a single estate in Ecuador were fed into a grinder to order. Slate boards, prices chalked on them, displayed croissants and cakes.

Kat, who had subsisted on coffee and fresh air for most of her adult life, was suddenly hungry. She ordered a flaky pain au chocolat.

"So," Charles said. "I suppose you're glad to be back home with Ross?"

"He's hardly been here," Kat said ruefully.

Charles' glance was knowing. "Of course. Anwen sent him to Bermuda, and then there's the stag party. I suppose he's a bit embarrassed as well. He'd hoped to bring you back from Bazakistan sooner, but his negotiation tactics didn't work."

Kat froze. "What tactics were those?"

"Based on poker," Charles said. "He called their bluff and said he wouldn't pay."

Hastily, he added, "He didn't mean a word of it, I can assure you. They wanted ten million for you, though, and Ross was going to struggle to lay his hands on that within a week. Why, even Dee couldn't do it."

"Really? Hasn't she made a fortune from online yoga?" Kat asked, not really interested in Dee, but hoping to draw the conversation away from Ross. Inwardly, she fumed at being treated like a pawn in a card game.

"Yes, her business is massive," Charles said. "Dee built it from nothing, you know. When she left school, she worked as an aerobics instructor and personal trainer. She was smart enough to see a market for videos and DVDs, and now online streaming."

"How inspirational," Kat said.

There was palpable pride in Charles' voice as he talked about Dee. Kat was surprised. Ross never spoke about her in that tone. "I guess you still see a lot of Dee?" she asked.

"Not as much as I'd like," Charles said. "Amy wouldn't want me to say this, and I'm very fond of her mother, naturally, but Dee was the love of my life. I behaved badly towards her, and she's punishing me for it now." He sighed. "I've only seen her and George on a handful of occasions since his birth. She's agreed to a visit today merely because Amy's travelled a hundred miles to see them."

"Why aren't you talking like this to Dee?" Kat asked, feeling awkward in her role as Charles' confessor. On impulse, she pulled the diamond engagement ring off her finger. "Propose marriage to her if that's the way you feel about her."

He laughed. "That's what all you girls want, is it?"

"Sometimes it's the right thing to do," she said. Other times, it wasn't. "Go on, take the ring. As long as it's back before Ross, what's the harm?"

"Nothing ventured, nothing gained," Charles said. He glanced at the door. "Is that Amy? We'd better be off to Primrose Hill."

His daughter arrived, hangover apparently banished. She was clutching a bunch of white roses in a supermarket bag.

"Ready?" Charles asked, hugging Amy.

Kat winked at him.

Chapter 38 **Kat**

Kat gave them two hours before texting Amy. "What did Dee say?" she asked.

Amy texted back, "She's thinking about it. How did you know?"

Kat grinned. She didn't really care, actually, whether the ring was returned promptly or not.

She hadn't told Amy everything about Bazakistan. Until her abduction, she'd thought Ross was crazy about her. He'd support her, no matter what happened. Ken and Ulan had seemed convinced Ross wouldn't pay her ransom, though. Of course, as soon as she'd told Ross afterwards, he'd denied it outright. He'd said it was a misunderstanding. It was odd that misunderstandings, like the existence of Amy's baby brother, so often turned out to be true.

Marriage suited some couples, like her parents. It might suit Charles and Dee. Anyone could see he loved her. When you found the right partner, it was for life.

If you harboured the tiniest seed of doubt about your lover, though, you'd be a fool to tie yourself to them forever. It didn't matter how rich, clever and handsome they were; how treacherous your emotions when you looked into their deep blue eyes. Kat thought of that seed growing first into a sapling, then a tree, its tendrils seizing and strangling the love in a marriage.

When Charles returned the ring, she would pawn it. She began to consider what her other possessions would fetch. There was a wardrobe full of designer dresses that would sell easily. Regretfully, Kat recalled the beautiful, filmy fabrics, and the fun she'd had on each champagne-fuelled night when she'd worn them. Later, she would make sure to show them off to Amy and take a few selfies. The memories would see her through hard times. She'd been poor before, and now, when she left Ross, she'd be poor again. It wouldn't last forever, though. Charles might even decide he owed her a favour, and invest in her new business.

Once her goods were sold, she'd use the cash to train as a distiller. After all, she could make vodka anywhere. Marty had taught her that. One day, Kat's very own premium vodka brand would rival Snow Mountain.

The doorbell rang. Kat switched on the intercom.

"It's Amy," a familiar voice said.

"Great," Kat replied. "I'm glad you've left the lovebirds behind. Wait down there. We'll go to Charlotte Street and you can give me the latest."

She still had plenty to tell Amy, too. Donning her spikiest stilettos before leaving the flat, Kat used the lift's mirrored walls to apply her brightest lipstick.

"I know a bar that does a mean vodka martini," she told Amy. "Coming?"

Thank you for reading **The Vodka Trail** - I hope you enjoyed it! I'd really appreciate it if you'd tell your friends by leaving a review on Amazon, Goodreads, or your blog.

I'd love to stay in touch with you, too. If you sign up for my newsletter at http://aaabbott.co.uk, I'll send you a free e-book of short stories. You'll also receive news about forthcoming books and live fiction events. I hope you can get to one; it would be wonderful to meet you.

You can also find me on Twitter (@AAAbbottStories) and Facebook.

Lightning Source UK Ltd.
Milton Keynes UK
UKOW01f2116170716

278532UK00002B/21/P